Katie almost gasped when she came out onstage for her solo and saw Sam, first row, center seat, as though he hadn't missed a single show.

She felt her heart pounding, and from the way his eyes brightened, he'd noticed the effect his presence had on her, too. The grin he tried to hide sent her pulse racing. And her number tonight was a love ballad. How in the world was she going to get through it?

The first note was a little shaky, but Katie managed to relax her throat and sing without choking. However, no matter how hard she tried, she couldn't keep her eyes from drifting his way before she left the stage. Warmth washed over her at the expression in his brown eyes. So convincing. If he wasn't in love with her, he should have been on the stage himself.

FRANCES DEVINE spent most of her childhood, teen, and young adult years in Dallas, Texas, but lived for five years in a little country community called Brushy Creek among the beautiful pinewoods of East Texas. There, she wrote her first story at the age of nine. She moved to Southwest Missouri more than twenty years ago and fell in love with the hills, the fall colors, and Silver Dollar City. Frances considers herself blessed to have the opportunity to write for Barbour. She is the mother of seven adult children and has fourteen wonderful grandchildren. Frances is happy to hear from her fans. E-mail her at fd1440writes@aol.com.

A Girl Like That

Frances Devine

Heartsong Presents

Dedicated with love to my son Rod Devine and my grand-daughter Robyn, who took care of everything and put up with me while I was writing this book.

To Tracey, who stayed with me at the hospital for several days, polished this up for me, and sent it to Barbour so I wouldn't miss my deadline. Love you, sweetheart. Many thanks.

Also to Steve, Sandy, Linda, Jack, and Bill, who helped in other ways. I love you more than I can say.

And you, too, Angie.

To my precious grandchildren and great-grandchildren. You are my angels.

To the Hughes Center Gang and the prayer warriors at Lebanon Family Church. Thanks for your prayers.

Special thanks to Carol Maniaci for praying me through it all.

A note from the Author:
I love to hear from my readers! You may correspond with me by writing:

Frances Devine
Author Relations
PO Box 721
Uhrichsville, OH 44683

ISBN 978-1-60260-355-4

A GIRL LIKE THAT

one

Chicago, May 1871

Katie O'Shannon stood on the platform and faced the teeming crowd waiting to board the train. The train from which she had just disembarked. She took a wobbly step forward then stopped short as loud shouts and excited greetings assaulted her ears. Sounds she'd longed for after four years on the farm. And yet, a twinge of fear in her stomach made her wonder if she'd been away from the city for too long. *Turn around, Katie. Smile at the friendly conductor and return to your nice, safe seat.*

Before she could take her own advice, the conductor cleared his gravelly throat. "Move along, miss. Others are waiting to disembark."

Katie's face turned feverish with embarrassment as she glanced over her shoulder into the frowning face of a tall man with bushy gray eyebrows and a curly mustache. "S–Sorry, sir." She gulped a deep, determined breath, clutched her reticule tightly, thankful she'd sent her trunk on ahead, and stepped forward.

To her surprise and relief, the crowd parted. She cleared the throng and glanced around for her father as she walked toward the depot.

Her Irish temper flared as she realized he was nowhere to be seen in one direction. She whipped about on her booted heel. Before she could begin her search, she slammed into a rock-hard wall. No, not a wall. In a beat of confusion, she felt a pair of strong hands grasping her arms, steadying her. Gasping, she stared at dark brown eyes, shadowed with annoyance, looking down at her from a strong, handsome face. "Saints preserve us,

5

I've got to learn to watch where I'm going."

For a second, his eyes seemed to soften. But he gave an abrupt nod, followed by a hasty departure as he shoved past her.

Katie's face flamed. Not five minutes in Chicago and she'd already behaved like a country bumpkin. Still, he needn't have been so rude. She glanced around, relieved to see that no one seemed to have noticed the incident.

"Katie. Katie O'Shannon!"

The next moment, she found herself enveloped in Michael O'Shannon's sturdy, comforting arms.

"Pa, I thought you forgot all about me!" She snuggled into the tobacco and peppermint smell of him and looked into his beaming face.

"What are you talking about? How could I forget my little girl? But for the life of me, I can't understand why you'd want to leave your grandfather Mason's nice, quiet farm and come to this crowded, filthy city."

Katie laughed. "That's just it. The farm is too quiet. Besides, I missed you, Pa." She squeezed his arm and threw him a saucy grin.

He winked and tweaked her nose as though she were still a child. "Now don't you go telling me lies, Katherine O'Shannon. It's the excitement of show business you've been missing. But don't you be getting any ideas about acting onstage, because I'll not have it. Just because you're eighteen now doesn't mean you can do as you please." The twinkle in his eyes belied the gruff voice, but Katie knew he meant his words.

She was spared the problem of replying as they reached a three-seated conveyance with HARRIGAN's written on the side. An ancient horse snorted and pawed the dirt.

"Sorry about this monstrosity, my girl. The regular carriage wasn't available."

Katie scrunched up her nose as she climbed in and sat on the cracked leather seat. "What's that awful smell?"

"Ah, we've been having an outbreak of fires for going on a

month now. It's been dry for spring." Michael took the reins, and they moved down the street amid the *clip-clop* of horses' hooves on the wooden street.

Katie glanced nervously at the wood structures lined on each side of the street.

"Don't you be worrying now, Katie girl." Michael puffed his lips. "It's a fine fire department we have these days."

"Oh, I'm not worried. I'm much too happy to worry. How far is it to the theater? Can we go there first?" Katie restrained herself from craning her neck to take in all the sights. After all, she was a grown woman. And regardless of her foolish moment of doubt as she disembarked, she was thrilled to be in Chicago, noise and all.

Michael gave her a sideways glance, and a smile puckered his lips. "Well, I guess we can, since I have a show in thirty minutes."

They pulled up in front of a two-story green and white wooden structure. Across the top hung a sign bearing the title, HARRIGAN'S MUSIC HALL AND THEATER, in bold letters.

Katie's stomach lurched with excitement. This was the moment she'd waited for since she was fourteen, when her father, newly widowed, had taken her from the exciting vaudeville scene of New York City and dropped her at her grandparents' farm in southern Illinois. She'd watched, lonely and feeling abandoned, as he snapped the reins and drove away to find work. Pulling herself from the unwelcome thoughts, Katie took her father's hand and stepped down onto the board sidewalk.

Immediately, a boy appeared at her father's elbow and took the reins. Vendors, pushing carts down the street, hawked their wares while dodging hansom cabs and other traffic.

Katie followed her father around to the side and entered the building.

A green-vested man looked up from his newspaper and grinned. "So this is the lovely Katie O'Shannon we've all been hearing about." He stood and gave Katie an elegant bow.

"It is, Thomas Harrigan, and you'll be keeping your distance." Michael gave the man a good-natured glare, which was returned with laughter.

"Katie, this rogue you see standing here is the theater owner and manager of the troupe. And he's really not a bad sort."

"It's very nice to meet you, sir." Katie offered her hand, which he took gently.

"And it's nice to meet you, my dear." He smiled then turned to Michael. "You didn't tell me she was a beauty and had a voice like an angel."

"No, and you can forget it. My daughter won't be performing in this show or any other."

Thomas twisted his mustache, looking her up and down in a way that made Katie feel like a thoroughbred filly. He took in a deep breath and shook his head with regret. "It's a crying shame, my friend."

Michael set his jaw. "That's a matter of opinion, and yours doesn't count where my girl's concerned. Come, daughter. I'll take you to a seat where you can watch the show. I have to get into costume." Michael took her hand and led her through a door into a large auditorium, already filled with people.

Ten minutes later, Katie sat mesmerized as house lights lowered and the curtain came up. The smell of grease paint tickled her nostrils, and the bright, shiny costumes filled her eyes with stars, bringing back sweet memories. But soon her nostalgia became lost in the excitement of the moment, as Katie laughed with the other afternoon theater patrons at the hilarious musical comedy.

As a young man with dark brown eyes sang a love song, the eyes of the man at the train station intruded upon Katie's thoughts. Her eyes drifted shut as suddenly she became the female lead and the handsome stranger sang to her in perfect baritone. Lost in the ebb and flow of the scene playing in her head, she started as applause flooded the packed theater. Her eyes flew open, but in her heart, the applause was for her.

Her heart thudded to the rhythm of the boisterous clapping. If only her pa wasn't so stubborn. No matter. "Soon, it will be me up there," she promised herself. "I was born for this."

⊱

Sam Nelson stormed through the door of the Nelson Law Firm and tossed his hat onto the rack in the corner.

Several desks were scattered around the room, all but his own occupied by harried-looking young men. Some were bright, overworked attorneys just grateful for a job in the illustrious firm founded by Sam's father. Others, like Charlie Jenkins, held lesser positions, but important nonetheless.

The secretary looked up from his desk in the corner. "Your father is waiting for you, sir."

"Thanks, Charlie. I'm sure he is. I'm an hour late."

But I wouldn't have been, he thought. Not if Harvey Simons had arrived on time. Harvey, a witness in one of the elder Mr. Nelson's cases, had taken a later train than he'd promised, throwing off Sam's schedule for the day. By the time Harvey's train arrived, Sam's temper was sharp enough to cut leather.

Sam thought of the lovely, golden-haired young woman he had brushed aside at the train station. Judging from her clothing and the uncertain smile of apology, she was fresh off the farm. He'd regretted his abruptness immediately and had gone back to apologize, but she'd already disappeared, lost in the crowd. He would have liked to have made amends to her, but it couldn't be helped. And he had no time to dwell on an unfortunate situation over which he had no control.

When he walked into his father's office, Eugene Nelson looked up from a sheaf of papers he was riffling through. "I'm pleased you could finally join me."

"Sorry, Father, but—"

"Never mind. You're here now." He bit the end off a cigar and puffed loudly as the flame from the match flared. "I have a case for you."

"What is it this time?" Probably another squabble over property lines or something just as trivial. Even after five years of working for his father, the elder Mr. Nelson treated Sam's efforts as though he were still a boy learning his ABCs.

"Jeremiah Howard has retained us for an injury case involving an Irish immigrant. I'd intended to give it to Bob, but he has a family emergency and won't be back for several weeks." He looked at his son through narrowed eyes. "This could be important for you. Do the job right, and it could push you up the ladder. You know what I mean."

Sam knew what he meant, all right. There was one position open for junior partner. Three young lawyers, including Sam, were gunning for it. And his father wasn't one to play favorites. If anything, Sam was expected to work harder and be smarter than anyone else. Sam had started at the bottom like everyone else, and it was up to his own efforts and abilities to rise to the top.

Sam flopped into the leather armchair in front of his father's desk. "Details?"

His father shoved a file folder toward him. "It's all here. Howard wants to get it settled before the end of the year."

Sam took the folder, left his father's office, and went to his desk. He leaned back for a moment, inhaling the smells of leather, old books, and cigar smoke. Smells he loved, familiar to him from his childhood.

He skimmed through the papers then returned to the first page and began to peruse the information.

One Chauncey Flannigan, an Irish immigrant employed at Howard's Warehouse and Lumberyard, had been involved in an accident while performing his duties. A large stack of lumber had slipped and tumbled down on the employee, knocking him to the floor.

According to Mr. Howard, who had been on the premises at the time, Flannigan had suffered nothing but a few scratches and scrapes. He'd been sent home for the rest of the day. When the man failed to return to work the following morning, Mr. Howard had naturally hired a man to replace him.

Two weeks later, bandaged and on crutches, Flannigan had shown up at Mr. Howard's office. He had just been released from the hospital, where he had undergone surgery for a head injury. He had also been treated for several broken bones. He claimed the injuries were a result of the incident at work and demanded restitution. Mr. Howard, the firm's long-standing client, denied the claim.

Within the file were two signed affidavits from witnesses claiming to have seen Flannigan at a tavern the night of the accident. The witnesses claimed there had been a fight. There was also a letter, signed by the foreman and several employees of the lumberyard, stating that Flannigan's injuries from the accident were minor and he'd left on his own two feet with no evidence of a head injury or broken bones.

Sam straightened the papers and leaned back. The case seemed open-and-shut to him. A ne'er-do-well attempting to profit at someone else's expense. Of course, he'd visit the lumberyard and talk to the witnesses. He'd also pay a visit to Chauncey Flannigan. That way he wouldn't be surprised by something detrimental to his client on court day.

"Hey, Sam." Jack Myers, one of the junior partners and Sam's friend, stood in front of Sam's desk.

"Hi. What's going on, Jack?"

"Just wanted to see you working on the case that's going to win you a promotion."

Sam glanced around the room, but no one seemed to have overheard. "It's not mine yet."

Jack laughed. "Okay. Actually, I wanted to see if you were busy tonight. Sally's cousin Janet is in town, and we need you to make it a foursome for dinner."

"Sure. Where do I pick her up and what time?"

"I thought we'd go together to pick up the girls. Meet me at my place around seven."

Sam nodded and watched with a twinge of envy as his friend went, whistling, back to his office. A small office, true. But at least it was Jack's alone.

Sam glanced down at the stack of papers on his desk. Maybe he shouldn't have accepted the invitation to dinner. He should probably be spending every minute on this case. But, after all, he needed to eat. And a little relaxation with a young woman wouldn't hurt either. Maybe it would help him forget the pair of brilliant blue eyes staring up at him from a face momentarily washed over with embarrassment. Embarrassment he was responsible for.

Sam shook his head. There was nothing he could do about that. And since it was unlikely he'd ever see the girl again, why did the memory keep intruding into his thoughts?

He leaned forward and started once more at the beginning of the first page. Yes. Cut-and-dried.

One corner of Sam's mouth turned up in a smile of satisfaction. The position of junior partner was right around the corner.

two

Ma Casey's dining room rang with laughter.

"Yes, it canna' be denied. Bobby Brown is a fine young lad, and he most definitely has taken a shine to our Katie girl."

Katie laughed at the good-natured bantering and turned her attention to the teasing Pat Devine. Old enough to be her grandfather, he'd taken it upon himself to tease her unmercifully and almost continuously for the entire month she'd been in Chicago.

She loved everything about this city. The theater. The boisterous troupe. Celebration parties at the boardinghouse after a successful night. And the bantering. But most of all, she loved the familiar feel of show business and show people. If only her mother were here, everything would be perfect again.

With a toss of her head, she shoved the pain away and planted her hands on her hips. She tossed Pat a fake scowl. "And what business is it of yours, mister, if he has? And what business would it be of yours if I returned his affection? Which I don't."

The room exploded with another round of laughter. It was no secret that Bobby Brown, one of the stagehands, was sweet on her, but she'd told him in no uncertain terms she wasn't interested. And it had nothing to do with the handsome face of the man from the station that continued to invade her thoughts and had even slid its way into her dreams once or twice.

"All right now. That's enough harping on my daughter." Michael's booming voice got their attention. "Come on now, it's almost noon. We need to get to the theater."

13

Father coming to her rescue, as always. Although, Katie was plenty able to hold her own with this rowdy crew. She'd been embarrassed and confused the first few days among the Irish troupe but had quickly come to realize their teasing was all in fun. The entire troupe had taken her under their wing, so she might as well get used to it.

Katie picked up her dishes and took them into the kitchen.

Ma Casey took them from her with a gentle smile. "They don't mean any harm. Don't you be paying them any mind now."

"I won't, Ma. Thanks for the wonderful meal. The oat cakes were the best I've ever eaten."

"Ah, go on with you." The tall, robust woman, who took care of them all, gave Katie a swat on the backside with her dish towel.

One by one, the members of the Irish troupe got up and cleared their dishes from the table. Gathering their things together, they headed out the door.

Katie always found this moment exciting. This was when her day really began.

Turning a deaf ear to Katie's own pleading, Father still thwarted the manager's attempts to add Katie to the cast of the show. But he'd reluctantly agreed she could work backstage until she found other means of employment.

Katie was happy to at least be working at the theater, but she had in no way given up her dream.

As she walked the five short blocks to the theater, she noticed the smell of smoke seemed stronger today. "Father, do you think there was another fire last night? My throat burns, and the smell is awful."

"It wouldn't surprise me, sweetheart. But look at the sky. Rain clouds are coming in. That'll put an end to the fires."

Hardly a day passed that at least one fire didn't break out somewhere in the rain-deprived city or surrounding area. The last letter from Katie's grandmother had revealed that rain had been almost as scarce in southern Illinois, and Gramps was getting a little worried about the crops.

As they neared the theater, a disturbance across the street drew Katie's attention.

A young man struggled to free himself from the tight grip of a patrolman. "Get your hands off me. I didn't do anything." The young man squirmed loose and took off running with the officer close behind.

The troupe had stopped, and Katie noticed the dark clouds upon their faces as they watched the incident.

"Another Irishman persecuted," Pa grumbled.

"Now, Michael, we don't know that. It looked to me like the man had stolen something." Rosie Riley's voice was soft as she patted Michael's arm.

"And why, do you suppose, would that be? They're starving down there in Conley's Patch. Yes, and in all the other immigrant shacks across the city."

Katie followed the others into the theater. She caught her father's arm before he could step into the men's dressing room. "Father, what did you mean? Who is starving?"

"Never you mind, daughter. There's not a blessed thing we can do about it except be charitable whenever we're able." A shadow crossed her father's face as he looked absently at Katie. "Be getting to your work now."

Puzzled, Katie stood, hands on hips, as her father walked away. She stomped toward the women's dressing area, where she had been assigned to work. She knew who would tell her what she wanted to know. And she'd find out before the day was over.

Katie spent most of the day with needle in hand, mending costumes. After the afternoon show, she took a break and found Bobby Brown behind the stage repairing ropes. "Bobby, I have a question for you." She put on her sweetest smile for the young man. A twinge of guilt afflicted her, but she quickly pushed it aside. She couldn't help it if he liked her more than she liked him.

Staring at her with near adoration, Bobby jumped up. He was

a nice-looking young man, with blond curls and honest eyes.

Katie told him about the incident outside the theater. "Who is starving, and what is Conley's Patch?" she questioned.

"Irish immigrants," Bobby stated, his expression somber.

"What do you mean?" Katie stared at him. "Most of the folks in this troupe are immigrants, including my father. I don't understand."

Bobby scratched his ear. "These immigrants are different, Katie. They came in throngs after the potato famine. They weren't received very well. It was hard for them to find jobs in the beginning. Things are better now, employment-wise. But they're shamefully underpaid, and most live in shacks in communities that are called shantytowns."

Katie tapped her foot impatiently. "So, what about that Patch place?"

He took a deep breath. "Conley's Patch is the worst of them all. The crime rate is high, and poverty and sickness affect near about every family. Some resort to stealing just to keep their families from starving."

"But isn't there some sort of aid for them?" Katie's heart picked up rhythm at the very thought of those poor people. "Surely they aren't just ignored."

"Of course. There are a number of societies that provide food and medical attention. But most of the folks who live there are too proud to take charity except in dire circumstances."

Sleep evaded Katie that night as she tossed and turned on the soft feather bed. How could a whole group of people be treated so badly? Especially right here in America. What if she could do something to help?

ತ

"So. You're mooning over a girl you saw once for thirty seconds." Jack shook his head and grinned across the table at Sam. "That must have been some meeting."

"I wouldn't exactly call it mooning," Sam retorted, stirring sugar into his coffee. "Of course I noticed her. She was beautiful. And it's only natural I'd think of her now and then, because of my conscience at the way I treated her."

"Oh, I see," Jack said with a chuckle. "It's your conscience that's preventing you from pursuing the lovely Janet, who has made it fairly plain she wouldn't find said pursuit distasteful."

Sam tossed his friend a sheepish look. "I know. You're right. So. . .you think Janet's interested?"

"Good. You're coming to your senses," Jack said. "Of course she's interested. Want me to set up another double date?"

Sam couldn't honestly say he was all that interested in the pretty young woman, but she was a nice diversion from his hectic life. "I guess. But don't make her any promises on my behalf."

"Would I do anything like that?"

"Yes, so don't. I don't mind taking her to dinner or the theater, but marriage to a stuffy socialite is out of the question."

"Isn't that sort of reverse snobbery?"

Sam shrugged. "Call it what you wish." He wasn't sure exactly why the young women in his parents' circle of friends had never appealed to him.

Jack grinned again. "All right, I'll leave out the proposal of matrimony when I send her the invitation to dinner and a show."

Sam turned his attention back to work. He had to finish some research for one of his father's senior partners before he could turn his attention to his own case. By early afternoon, he had completed his task and headed out to the hospital where Chauncey Flannigan had been treated.

Despite Sam's power of persuasion, the doctor who had performed Mr. Flannigan's surgery refused to speak with Sam without permission from Flannigan, so Sam left and went to the courthouse. After a few minutes with Judge Cohen, a friend of Sam's father, he returned to the hospital with a court order to release information to the Nelson Law Firm.

Dr. Voss sat, his eyes stormy, the lines of his face deep and forbidding as he stared across his desk. Without offering Sam a seat, he gave a detailed report on Flannigan's injuries. According to the doctor, the head injury had been serious and, without surgery, could have been fatal. The other injuries involved a broken leg and wrist.

Sam gave him a grudging nod and turned toward the door to leave.

The sound of the doctor's voice stopped him short. "The conditions at the warehouses and lumberyards are appalling. And the mills are even worse. Why the owners won't do something about it is beyond my understanding. The cost would be nothing compared to the bodily harm inflicted."

Sam eyed the doctor who, it seemed, was hostile to Jeremiah Howard. "There are those who say Mr. Flannigan's injuries have nothing to do with the lumberyard."

The look of surprise on the doctor's face couldn't have been fabricated. "What else could have caused it?"

"There are witnesses who have stated there were only minor injuries from the accident at the lumberyard. There are also witnesses who claim the major injuries were the result of a tavern brawl."

He stared at Sam. "That's ridiculous. Mr. Flannigan came to me unconscious. And not from any tavern."

"Are you sure about that?"

"His neighbor carried him across his back for miles. Neither was drunk nor appeared to have been in a fight. His injuries are consistent with an accident."

"Then are you prepared to swear on oath that Flannigan's injuries could only have been inflicted by the incident at work?"

"Well. . ." The doctor hesitated. "Of course, I didn't actually see the accident."

"When did Flannigan arrive at the hospital, Dr. Voss?"

"The morning after the accident. His wife had been trying to get him to come since the night before, but he wouldn't hear of it. No money. When Mrs. Flannigan couldn't wake him the next morning, she banged on the neighbor's door."

Sam couldn't deny the doctor sounded convincing. But the doctor didn't deal with liars and cheats every day the way an attorney did. Sam's evidence came from witnesses. The doctor was only guessing. "I see." Sam wrote in his notebook. "Then you can't be certain the injuries didn't occur at the tavern the night of the accident, as the witnesses have stated."

"Well, no, but. . ."

"Thank you, doctor. You've been very helpful." Sam tucked the pencil into his breast pocket.

The doctor stepped forward as Sam started to walk out the door. With a pained look on his face, he spoke. "Maybe I can't swear to what happened. But I believe with everything in me that Flannigan is speaking the truth. This isn't the first time I've had to treat injuries that occurred at one of Howard's places of business."

"I'm sure it isn't," Sam said. "Injuries happen every day. I wouldn't want your job."

"And I wouldn't want yours, young man."

Sam, his confidence a little shaken, stared in surprise as the doctor turned away. Why was the man so sure of Flannigan's innocence? He shrugged and left the hospital. The injured man must be a good actor. But then, most con men were.

He returned to the office and looked over the witness affidavits. They were definitely legal. And what reason would the men have to lie?

He finished up his work for the day and went home to get ready for a visit to Sally Reynolds's house to see Janet. As he dressed, he tried to remember what the young woman looked like. He remembered her auburn hair and a rather annoying laugh, but when he tried to remember her eyes, all he could see were the brilliant blue eyes of the girl at the crowded depot.

Shaking himself free from the memory, Sam walked out

the door. He would get to know Janet better. Who knew? Maybe she wasn't like other girls in their social set.

Four hours later, he stood in his bedroom once more, changing into pajamas and robe. His evening with Janet had been pleasant. She was a nice girl and very entertaining. But she chattered incessantly. He sighed, wishing he had stayed home and done some more reviewing of the Flannigan case.

He went to open his window and noticed a pink sky in the distance. Another fire. This time in the direction of the river. He hoped some family hadn't lost their home tonight. The sky had been cloudy that morning, promising rain, but hopes were dashed when the sun had come out before noon.

He extinguished the overhead gaslight and climbed into bed. His mind began to go over plans for the following day. He yawned and closed his eyes. The sound of Dr. Voss's angry voice seemed to shout into his brain. Sam knew it was time he met the man who'd instilled such loyalty into the doctor. Very soon, he intended to pay a visit to Chauncey Flannigan.

three

The clatter of dishes and the aroma of cabbage and onions assailed Katie as she ladled out bowl after bowl of hot soup.

The kitchen had opened at noon, and two hours later, the line still coiled through the door and down the wooden sidewalk outside. Mrs. Carter, the director and, as it seemed to Katie, the most untiring worker, handed out thick slices of bread and words of encouragement to the downtrodden throng who passed through. Katie had learned that the Irish had no monopoly on poverty. The people who came here for food were of every race and nationality.

Katie had inquired about and found the location of this food kitchen three days ago, right after Bobby had told her of the existence of the charitable organizations. Mrs. Carter, happy to have another pair of hands, had put her to work on the spot. Katie could only work her days off at the theater, so this was her first day on the job.

A tall man with enormous arms and not a tooth in his mouth carried a full pot of soup from the kitchen. He grunted when Katie thanked him. He grabbed the empty pot and disappeared behind the door without a word.

Katie hoped there was plenty more soup back there. She didn't think she could stand to turn anyone away hungry.

A girl, who appeared to be around Katie's age or perhaps a little older, stepped up in front of Katie. Red curls escaped from the pulled-back bun and fell across an oval face. She lifted hazel eyes to Katie. "Miss, would it be at all possible for me to take a wee bit of food home to Ma and my little sister?" The girl's voice wasn't much more than a whisper and sounded weak.

"Why. . .I don't know. I suppose it would be all right."

Katie glanced at Mrs. Carter, who shook her head.

"But. . ."

The director sighed and spoke directly to the girl. "I'm sorry, dear. It's against the rules for us to send food off the premises. But, if you'll bring your family here, we'll be happy to give them something to eat."

An imploring, almost desperate look washed over the girl's face. "But you see, my sister is ill, and my ma would never be able to walk this far."

Regret crossed Mrs. Carter's countenance, and sympathy filled her eyes as she looked at the girl. "As I said, I'm not allowed to do that. Nothing can leave the premises."

A choked sound emitted from the girl's lips as she turned and walked away. As she reached the door, she stumbled then caught herself and stepped out on the sidewalk.

Katie swallowed around the knot in her throat and, without a word, handed her ladle to Mrs. Carter. Tearing off her apron, she tossed it onto a stool. "Sorry, I have to go after her. I'll return when I can." She threw the words over her shoulder as she hurried toward the door.

The girl was halfway down the street. Just as Katie started after her, she saw her sway and fall to the sidewalk. Pedestrians hurried past her, hardly slowing to even glance at the fallen girl.

With a cry of indignation, Katie pushed her way through the crowd and knelt beside the unconscious girl. Frightened, she rubbed the chapped hands and patted the pale face. "Come on now, wake up. Please." She felt the girl's pulse, relieved to find it strong.

"Wha. . . ? What happened?" The girl struggled to get up, and Katie took a firm grip on her arm and helped her to her feet.

"You fainted," Katie said, still holding on. "Have you been ill?"

"Oh. No, I'm just—" She stopped, a red flush washing over her face.

"When did you eat last?" Katie's no-nonsense tone seemed to calm the girl.

"I'm not sure. A couple of days ago, I think."

"Oh my goodness!" Katie, who had never skipped a meal in her life, couldn't imagine such a thing. "Come on, we'll fix that right now."

"No, no. I couldn't possibly eat anything when Ma and Betty are hungry. Betty had the last of the soup last night." She stopped and blushed again, apparently realizing she'd just shared personal information with a stranger. "I've been trying to find work, but no one wants to hire me."

"Well, you wouldn't be able to work if you did find employment. You're much too weak." Katie threw a quick prayer for wisdom up to heaven. How could she get some food into this girl without touching her pride? Noticing a small park bench at the end of the street, she guided the girl toward it and sat beside her. "I'm Katie O'Shannon," she said. "What is your name, if you don't mind my asking?"

"Bridget. Bridget Thornton."

"Listen, Bridget. The best thing you can do for your mother and sister is to get some nourishment into your body so that you'll have the strength to help them."

The girl sighed but said nothing.

"I'll tell you what. While you sit here and rest, I'll get you something to eat. Then we'll take some food to your home."

Katie's heart ached as she saw hunger and pride battle for predominance on the girl's face.

"All right," Bridget whispered. "I don't know what Ma will say, but I can't let them starve to death."

A half hour later, Katie and Bridget stepped out of a cab in front of a tiny, weathered shack—one among rows of the same lined up on either side of the narrow dirt street. Curious neighbors stared as Katie reached up and paid the carriage driver. Then they went inside.

The Thornton home was clean in spite of the evident

poverty. As the grateful mother and little sister ate, Katie learned from Bridget that the family had arrived from Ireland a year earlier.

"Things were na' so bad at first. Hard, but Da always made sure we had food on the table. Then, two months ago. . ." Bridget's eyes filled with tears as she continued. "A fire broke out in a house down by the river. Da went to help. He saved a woman and her three children. But he didn't make it out of the house." A sob caught her throat, and she stopped.

Katie knew the Thorntons weren't the only family in dire straits. She could see poverty and grief in every inch of Conley's Patch. She didn't know what she could do. But she knew she would do something.

⁂

The shacks were lined up so close they were almost touching on each side of the road. Between the rows, a canal running down the middle of the street carried waste of all kinds.

Sam looked on in disbelief, touching his fingers to his nose to ward off the stench of waste and garbage.

Chickens and children ran here and there. Raucous laughter rang out from somewhere up the street, and sounds of an argument proceeded from a house across the street from Chauncey Flannigan's.

Sam stepped up onto the ramshackle porch and knocked on the door. The sound of a chair scraping the floor assured Sam his knock had been heard.

The door swung open, and a woman just past her first youth stared at him. Her warm brown eyes held a questioning look.

Sam removed his hat. "Mrs. Flannigan?"

"Yes?"

"My name is Sam Nelson. Is your husband at home?"

"Who is it, Sarah?" The booming voice came from across the room.

Sarah turned. "A fellow by the name of Sam Nelson. He's wanting to see you."

"Well, what does he want?" The voice sounded impatient.

Mrs. Flannigan turned inquiring eyes to Sam. "And what would you be wanting, sir?"

Amused, Sam answered, "Please tell your husband I'm an attorney and wish to speak with him about his injuries."

"He says—"

"I heard him. Let him in."

The tiny woman stood aside and allowed Sam to pass into the room.

Whereas the outside of the home had been little more than a shack, Mrs. Flannigan had apparently tried to turn the inside into something resembling a cozy home. Clean, crisp curtains hung on the lone window looking out at the filthy street. The worn, broken plank floor was brushed clean, and the walls shone as though they had been freshly scrubbed. It was obvious the Flannigans had seen better times, for a cuckoo clock hung upon the wall over the fireplace and several porcelain knickknacks held places of importance on the mantle.

Chauncey Flannigan was rugged, or he would have been had the color not been drained from his sunken cheeks and his eyes not circled with dark rings that marked nights of worry. His thin body bespoke more than a few missed meals. His dark brown eyes squinted with suspicion from the sofa on which he sat. A crutch leaned against the wall beside him, and something steamed from the mug he held.

He motioned for Sam to sit on a nearby chair. "What can I do for you, Mr. Nelson? I can't afford a lawyer, so if it's me business you're after, I'm afraid you're wasting your time." He raised his eyebrows, questioning.

"As a matter of fact, Mr. Flannigan, I'm not here to solicit you as a client. Our firm has been retained by Jeremiah Howard."

For a fraction of a moment, a scowl appeared on Flannigan's face. "I see. Howard is still determined not to pay my hospital bills. I'd hoped he might be having a conscience in there somewhere and just maybe he'd be changing his mind."

"Ungrateful wretch of a man," Flannigan's wife said as she stood over a pot at the stove. She seemed not to be speaking to the men at all. "After Chauncey never missed a day of work. Not even when he had pneumonia."

"Please, Sarah, let me speak with Mr. Nelson."

She turned innocent eyes on her husband. "And who's stopping you? I was just stating my opinion."

Sam hid his grin beneath a cough. He opened his briefcase and pulled out a copy of the witnesses' statements, having left out the names for the sake of privacy. He handed the papers to Flannigan.

The injured man glanced through the papers, and confusion filled his eyes. "But why would anyone be saying such things about me?" He looked at Sam and shook his head. "I can't imagine, sir. But I wouldn't darken the door of a tavern. My Sarah would have my hide."

"And ain't that the truth of it?" the woman said, stirring her pot. "What are they sayin' about you, Chauncey?"

"That I left the lumberyard with only a few scrapes and bruises."

She gasped, turning, the ladle in her hand like a scepter. "Chauncey Flannigan leaving his job over a few scrapes and bruises? Losing wages? Taking food out of his children's mouths over a few scrapes and bruises? Never. It's a pack of lies."

"Well, Mrs. Flannigan, my client doesn't think they are lies. And I haven't found any evidence that they're anything but the truth."

"So that's the way the land lies." Flannigan's voice took on a hard note. "I'll be saying good-bye to you now, sir. But let me tell you this. I'm an honest man. And I'll not sit by and let a bunch of greedy liars, paid off by Howard, ruin my good name." He thrust the papers back at Sam. "You can be showing yourself to the door."

Sam slipped the papers back into his briefcase and left.

He stood on the porch for a moment, glancing around at the neighborhood. A wave of nausea arose in his throat. How could people live like this? His breath caught as he glanced at the house next to the Flannigans'.

The young woman from the train station stood knocking on the rickety door, a cloth-covered basket on her arm. She turned and absently glanced in his direction, and a startled look of recognition crossed her face.

A sudden puff of wind caught at the napkin, and it flew off the basket and down the steps.

As if instinct took over, Sam ran to the napkin, which had stopped just before reaching the filthy canal. He picked it up and walked to the side of the porch where she stood, her eyes wide. He grinned as he handed her the cloth. "I doubt you'll want this now, but here it is."

"Thank you, sir," she said, taking the napkin by one corner. "It will wash."

Sam cleared his throat. "I don't know if you remember me. We ran into each other at the train station a couple of months ago."

"I remember," she murmured, lowering her eyes.

"Well. . ." *Get it out, Sam. Since when were you ever tongue-tied in the presence of a beautiful woman?* "I'd like to apologize for my manners. I was in a terrible hurry, but that's no excuse to be rude. Especially to a lady."

As Sam stood with bated breath, the girl raised her beautiful eyes to him and flashed him a smile that seemed to light up everything in Sam's line of vision. "I forgive you, sir."

The door jerked open. "Katie, I knew you'd come today!" A laughing little girl grabbed the young woman's hand, dragged her inside, and slammed the door.

Sam took one impulsive step forward, tempted to climb the steps and knock. Then he stopped. Of course he couldn't do any such thing.

He walked to his buggy and untied the horse. So the girl

of his dreams was an Irish immigrant from shantytown. That rather surprised him. But at least now he could put a name to the face that haunted his every waking moment. *Katie. Katie.*

He drove away from Conley's Point, musing. *Now I know where to find you, Katie girl. So don't be surprised if you see me again very soon.*

four

"No, no, and a thousand times no."

Katie bit her lip as her pa's voice boomed across the stage and through the empty theater. He stood nose to nose with Thomas Harrigan, and for a moment, Katie thought he might strike the manager.

"Michael, would you be seeing my point of view for one little moment?" Harrigan's voice of reason hadn't gotten through to Katie's irate pa so far. "I'm not asking for her to be part of the show. Just one song before the first act."

"One song? Not even one line. I've been telling you my daughter won't be part of the troupe. And that's the end of the matter."

Katie's heart sank at the finality of his words. From experience, she knew he meant what he said. Still, she couldn't let this opportunity pass without at least trying to change his stubborn mind. "Father, would you just listen?" Katie tugged on his hand until he glared at her.

"Don't be wheedling at me, Katie O'Shannon. I've said my piece, and I'll not be changing my mind." His features wrinkled in anger. "No daughter of mine is going to kill herself performing day after day and night after night."

Surprised, Katie stared as her pa's eyes flooded with moisture. Angrily, he rubbed a fist across his eyes and stomped off the stage.

So that was it? He believed the stage had caused her mother's illness and death? But. . .she died of pneumonia.

Katie squared her shoulders. She'd talk to him later. This wasn't the end of it.

"Well, as he said, I guess that's that." Mr. Harrigan threw

her a regretful glance and then walked toward the wings.

"Don't be too sure about that," Katie called after him. "I'm not giving up yet."

The tenor who usually performed before the first act had received a better offer, packed up his things, and left with about an hour's notice. Mr. Harrigan had hoped Katie's father would let her fill in until he could find a replacement.

Determined to reason with Pa, Katie hurried backstage. She glanced around and saw him near the dressing rooms talking to Rosie. Their backs to her, she stopped as she heard her father speak her name.

"I'm not going to let her get mixed up in it, Rosie. Not my Katie. Her mother, bless her soul, wanted something better for her. And so do I."

"Now, Michael, I understand your wantin' a better life for Katie, although show business isn't so bad, as far as I can tell. But you're only going to push her into it if you don't stop being so stubborn. Let the girl sing for a couple of weeks until Thomas finds someone. Maybe that'll be enough to get the theater out of her system."

Katie held her breath, waiting for her pa's response. Her heart jumped when she heard him heave a deep sigh.

"Ah, Rosie. It's a hard thing, it is, raisin' a girl without her mother." He sighed again. "I'd hoped she'd meet some young man and be pleased to wed by now."

Rosie's lips stretched into a grin. "I'm sure there's a young man or two here in Chicago who'd be happy to oblige. And the girl will more than likely be a wife soon enough. But, in the meantime, let her sing, Michael. What's the harm in it?"

"Do you really think so?"

Excitement clutched Katie's stomach. At last. A small sign of her pa's mind opening to reason.

"Yes, I really do."

Katie could have grabbed Rosie and hugged her. She bit her lip to keep from shouting.

"Well then, maybe I'll think about it." Without another word, he went into the men's dressing room.

Katie burst forward. "Rosie! Thank you."

The buxom redhead turned in surprise. "Katie O'Shannon, it's eavesdropping you are now?"

"Couldn't help myself. And it was well worth it." She sent the older woman a saucy grin.

"Don't be countin' your chicks before they're hatched, missy. He hasn't said yes."

"Yet." Katie kissed Rosie on the cheek. "And don't you be trying to marry me off. I heard what you told Pa."

"Ah, I was only calmin' the man down. I'm still trying to get myself married off."

Katie was pretty sure she knew who Rosie wanted to marry but decided she'd best keep her lips buttoned. Her pa would have to realize Rosie's worth on his own.

"Thanks for reasoning with him. I want to be on that stage. I want it so badly."

"I know you do. But remember one thing—the new wears off, Katie. And youth wears off, too. Don't wait as long as I did to discover show business isn't enough to fill a person's heart forever."

The image of a handsome young man, running after a wayward napkin, flashed across Katie's mind. Her heart raced for a moment as she remembered the look on his face as he apologized for the incident at the train station.

Closing her mind to the memory, she sent Rosie a saucy grin. "I don't need any young man to make me happy. The theater is quite enough for me." But as a pair of dark brown eyes invaded her mind once more, a twinge of doubt bit at her heart.

She spent the rest of the morning mending costumes and arranging the unruly wigs that the dancers wore. The actresses, with their friendly banter, kept her laughing. She reveled in the backstage atmosphere and wanted nothing more than to be a real part of it all. If only Pa would change his mind.

One thing she was pretty sure of. The stage hadn't killed her mother. She'd been the picture of health and happiness until she came down with pneumonia.

At lunchtime, Mr. Harrigan called Katie to his office. His eyes danced as he ushered her in. Katie's stomach did a flip-flop when she saw her pa standing across the room. This was it. She knew it was.

"Katie, your father has generously decided to let you fill in until I find another singer to replace Roger." Before Katie could respond, the manager added, "He has a few conditions. So I'll let him take over from here."

"Yes, Pa?" Katie's voice shook with excitement as her father cleared his throat and stood frowning at them both.

"Here's the way of it," he said. "There'll be no revealing of the ankles nor of. . .anything else that would be indecent."

Katie's face heated from hairline to neckline. "Pa!"

Frowning, he raised his hand for silence. "I'll approve all costumes to make sure they are fittin' and proper for my daughter to wear. And I'll approve the songs you'll be singing to make sure they are decent and moral."

Indignation sparked. "As though I'd wear anything improper or sing an immoral song. Grandma would—" At her pa's scowl, Katie snapped her lips together.

He shook his finger at her. "Don't be interrupting me, young lady. I'm not finished." He turned a stern eye on her. "You're not to be accepting dinner invitations from any of the young bucks that're sure to be asking, and you don't go anywhere with anyone without my approval."

"Where would I go?" She scowled back.

His eyebrows rose, and she mentally stepped back. "Yes, Pa," she said with unaccustomed meekness.

Harrigan's eyes twinkled, and he winked at Katie. "All right then, Michael, is that it?"

"For now. If anything else comes to mind, I'll be letting you know."

"Sam, stop pacing and get down to whatever is bothering you." The older Mr. Nelson's impatient tone revealed his tiredness as he leaned back in his favorite leather chair in the library. Sam figured his father was stuffed from dinner and probably wanted nothing more than to close his eyes and doze off for a few minutes.

"Sorry, Father." Sam dropped into a chair across from his father, considering how to broach the subject. After all, several of their influential clients had business interests in or around Conley's Patch. "I met with Chauncey Flannigan today."

His father paused with a match halfway to his pipe. "You went to the Patch?" He struck the match to his pipe and then tossed it onto the clean hearth of the fireplace.

"Yes." Sam frowned as he watched the match burn down to ash.

"Well?"

"Have you been down there lately, Dad?"

"To shantytown?" He frowned at his son. "Why would I?"

Why would he indeed? Father's contributions to the poor were more in the manner of a few pennies in the offering plate variety. "Conditions are terrible. I saw children playing near an open ditch, containing garbage and human refuse, that ran down the middle of the street. The smell was horrible." Sam jumped up and began to pace again. "And that's not all. The housing is unspeakable. Hardly more than shacks for the people to live in."

Sam's father frowned. "What exactly are you trying to say, son?"

"Well, shouldn't something be done to help these people?"

"Sit down," his father commanded. "I refuse to speak with you while you are pacing the floor."

Once again, Sam dropped into the chair.

Mr. Nelson peered over the top of his steepled hands. "Sam,

your compassion for your fellow man is commendable, but I don't believe you understand this particular condition."

"What do you mean?"

He raised his palms and sighed. "These shanty Irish are a shiftless bunch. Lazy and slothful, not to mention deceitful and dishonest. Just look at this Flannigan character."

His father's voice stopped as though that settled the matter, but that far from satisfied Sam's concerns about an entire community living in such deplorable conditions. "Please continue."

"There really isn't much more to say about it. These people will take everything they can get and come back for more. You could put them in a mansion, and a year later, it would be in shambles. They have no pride and no gumption." He leaned forward and peered at Sam. "Trust me, son. There's nothing you can do for these people."

Sam knew better than to try to argue with his father. The man was a seasoned attorney, after all. He never lost an argument. There was no point in telling him about Sarah Flannigan's attempt at making a shack into a cozy home. There was no point in mentioning Chauncey Flannigan's outrage at being called anything less than a man of honor. He dropped the subject and excused himself.

Going out onto the veranda, he leaned against a pillar and gazed out into the night. A haze from recent fires hovered in the air. Most of them had taken place across the river, although a few had broken out in the city. And there was no getting away from the haze and smell of smoke in any part of Chicago.

Sam had overheard some of the employees at the office talking about their concerns. They feared if it didn't rain soon, conditions could only get worse.

Sam felt they were worrying unnecessarily. After all, Chicago now had a real fire department. The volunteers had been scattered all over town, and too often, homes and businesses had burned to the ground before they arrived. Yes, surely with the new fire department, Chicagoans could rest assured that they were in good hands.

Sam walked back inside and found his mother about to go upstairs. She lifted her cheek for his goodnight kiss. Reaching up, she brushed her hand across his forehead.

"Son, is anything bothering you?" She peered closer. "Or are you ill?"

Sam took her hand in his and smiled. "Nothing's wrong, Mother. You worry too much."

"A mother's duty." She gave a small sigh. "You do know I'm always willing to listen if you need to talk about anything."

"Of course, I know, Mother. Nothing's wrong. I promise." But as he watched her climb the stairs, he knew something was—if not wrong—different.

Grabbing his briefcase from the hall table, he went upstairs. He'd glance through the papers on the Flannigan case before he went to bed. But he had no reason to doubt his father's assurance that Flannigan was simply another Irish ne'er-do-well out to get something for nothing.

And yet, a twinge of doubt intruded into Sam's mind. Flannigan had been angry, but who wouldn't be under the circumstances? After all, Sam was a hostile attorney out to win the case for the other side. And he'd shown up at the Flannigans' home uninvited. The Flannigans had appeared to be poor but decent people.

What if his father was wrong? He'd admitted he hadn't even been to the Patch recently. So what did he base his judgment on? Was he so involved with his wealthy clients he couldn't see the other side at all? Or didn't want to? Sam brushed the idea away. He knew his father was an honest man. Still, a man could be honest and shortsighted at the same time, couldn't he? Even a man as great as his father.

The questions plagued him as his mind replayed the scene in the Flannigans' home, the living conditions in Conley's Patch.

He was a facts man and tried not to be ruled by emotions, so the letters of testimony by witnesses at the lumberyard should be all the evidence he needed. But something tugged at him. Something he couldn't quite put his finger on.

His heart picked up rhythm as an image flashed across his mind. Would he see her again if he went back to shantytown? Regardless of the outcome of this case, there was one thing Sam knew. The lovely young Irish girl with the golden curls and shining blue eyes couldn't possibly be lazy or shiftless. He'd bet his boots on that.

Uncertainty stabbed him sharply. *Lord, what should I do?*

Silence was his only answer. He couldn't really expect anything else. He hadn't spent time with God in a long time. And it had been months since he'd attended church.

A sudden wave of loneliness washed over Sam. He pushed it down and turned to his work.

❧

"Ladies and gentlemen, welcome to Harrigan's, where our one desire is to entertain to your delight and satisfaction. Our production of *The Golden Pipes* is nearing an end. We've only two more weeks, but never fear. There'll be another great production coming up before you know it." Thomas Harrigan's voice seemed to fade, and his frame became a blur.

Katie's legs felt like rubber as she stood in the wings awaiting her cue. *Oh God, please don't let me faint.*

"And now, ladies and gentlemen, I'm pleased to introduce a young lass with eyes as blue as the skies of Erin. But don't any of you fellows be getting any ideas. Because she has a proper Irish father with fists like mountains."

The roar of the laughing crowd startled Katie, and she stood up straight.

"So let's give a true Chicago welcome to Miss Katherine O'Shannon."

Katie walked onto the stage, propelled by sheer emotion.

Thomas gave her a smile and walked off, leaving her alone

on the suddenly unfamiliar stage.

As she faced the applauding audience, she could feel the brush of the curtains against her hair and she envisioned herself falling backward in a faint, ripping the curtain from the rope. *Stop it. Think of Mother and Father. Make them proud.*

Her lips curved in a faint smile, and she heard murmurs of approval from the people in front of her. The opening bars of her music floated to her ears. A surge of strength encouraged her, and she opened her lips and began to sing.

The next thing she knew, the last line of "A Little Bit of Heaven" trilled from her throat, and the audience was on its feet, applauding and cheering. Katie blushed, gave a little curtsy, and then hurried off the stage.

She fell into her father's arms. A wide grin split his face. "Go back, Katie girl. Sure and they're wanting more." He turned her and gave her a little shove.

Rejuvenated, she almost danced onto the stage and sang the last few lines of her song again. She floated off the stage and in a daze heard her friends congratulating her.

Katie watched the show from the wings, too excited to sit and too jittery to do any sewing. Over and over, she relived the performance and the wonderful reception the audience had given her.

That night, she repeated her number and was received with the same enthusiasm as she had before. By the time she and the troupe got back to the boardinghouse, she was so emotionally exhausted she practically stumbled through the door to her room. She went to bed convinced she wouldn't sleep a wink, but exhaustion won out and she quickly fell into a deep slumber.

≈

The next two weeks flew by for Katie. She loved performing her songs but secretly hoped her father would allow her to take a small part in the next musical comedy. She'd read it over and over and was mesmerized by the enchanting Maggie Donovan and her crooning suitor, Sean Kelly. All the major roles had been assigned, with Emma Gallagher getting the lead female role. Katie knew she wasn't ready for those anyway, but she had her eye on the one-line part of the housemaid, Rose. When she tried to broach the subject to her father, however, he threatened to pull her from the singing number if she brought up the subject again.

The first official rehearsal day was bittersweet for Katie. It was exciting to see the troupe walking around the stage practicing their parts. Her father had acquired the role of Sean Kelly's Uncle Andrew and had everyone in stitches in the boardinghouse living room as he became the bumbling Irish tavern keeper.

Patsy Brown had gotten the part Katie coveted and let everyone know she wasn't very happy with it. Katie felt like slapping the girl every time she heard the whining complaints. As she watched Patsy's rather insipid characterization of the young housemaid, Katie told herself she could have done a much better job.

They were beginning the second week of rehearsals when Rosie Riley tripped over a rope that had been left on the floor backstage. The doctor's proclamation of a broken foot set the cast astir.

Katie was just coming out of the ladies' dressing room when her father found her.

"Katie girl," he said, "it's against my better judgment, but the show opens next week, and someone has to take over for poor Rosie."

Katie's jaw dropped open. "Me? I get to take Rosie's part?"

"Well, of course not. And you having never played a show in your life? Patsy steps into the role of Maggie's cousin, Sally, and you get the part of the housemaid. But only until Rosie can walk again." He sighed, and worry crossed his face. "It's obvious you've got stars in your eyes and won't have peace until you give the stage a try. But Katie girl, I can't help but hope it'll wear off and someday you'll settle for a more normal life."

"Oh, but Father, I don't understand why it worries you so. You love show business yourself. And I know Mother did, too. I can still remember how her face would glow before she stepped onto the stage."

"Maybe so, but I'll always be blaming myself for taking her away from her parents' farm and into this crazy life. Maybe she wouldn't have gotten sick."

"Father, you don't know that. Why, just last year, little Annie Samson came down with pneumonia. She was only six years old and was gone in no time. People on farms get sick and pass away, too."

He cleared his throat and looked away, clearly finished with the current conversation. "Well now, you better get with Patsy and see if she can give you some tips about your part. You'll be needing a script, too." He kissed her and walked out of the dressing room.

Katie couldn't help the little scream of joy that escaped. She glanced around to make sure no one heard. She wouldn't want anyone to think she was glad Rosie broke her foot, because she certainly wasn't. But, oh, she was in a play! At last!

&

"I'm not handing out good money to some inexperienced clerk!" The tall, burly man sitting across from Sam's father was red-faced with anger. He leaned forward, and his eyes squinted at the elderly attorney.

"Mr. Howard, I can assure you my son is neither inexperienced nor is he a clerk." Sam could tell from the glint in his father's eyes that he was fast losing patience with Jeremiah Howard. "Sam is a bright young attorney who is being considered for partnership. He is well qualified to represent you."

"That's not good enough. I want a senior partner, and that's all there is to it."

"Yes, well, I'm sorry, but neither I nor the other senior partners are available. So if you do not wish to be represented by Sam, you're welcome to find yourself another attorney."

Sam, seated next to his client, almost laughed at the bevy of emotions crossing the man's beefy face.

Howard started to stand then dropped back into his chair and cleared his throat. "Well, all right. I suppose I can give the boy a chance."

Sam, in spite of his hopes that this case would win the partnership for him, was almost disappointed with Howard's decision. Everything about the man filled Sam with distaste. From the smell of his apparently unwashed body to the spittle that sprayed from his mouth when he talked. And this character was one of the wealthiest men in Chicago.

At a nod from his father, Sam stood. "I'll see you to the front, Mr. Howard. Our secretary will make an appointment for you to see me later this week, and we'll go over the case so you can see where we are in the legal process."

Howard hefted his form out of the chair. "An appointment won't be necessary. Let me know when to appear in court. I expect to win this case, Nelson. See to it."

Sam escorted his client to the front door and said goodbye. He wished he could put his foot on the man's backside and give a push. He neither liked nor trusted Mr. Howard. But liking his clients wasn't part of his job. If the man was innocent of wrongdoing as evidence seemed to support, he had a right to counsel.

As he was about to leave the office later that day, Jack hailed him. "How about a game of billiards tonight?"

"Billiards? Where?"

"My father just finished renovating two rooms on the third floor." He grinned. "Mother finally rebelled against the cigar smoke and loud voices of Father's cronies. He's calling tonight the grand opening. Nine o'clock?"

"Sure, I'll be there."

Sam wasn't sure what his own father would think of his plans. Isaiah Myers owned one of Chicago's more notorious taverns featuring dancing girls and backroom gambling. But Sam didn't see any harm in a game of billiards, especially since it was at the Myers home. Jack was a decent fellow and wouldn't have invited him if anything wasn't on the up-and-up.

When Sam was ushered into the third-floor room promptly at nine, cigar smoke nearly knocked him over.

Jack waved from across the crowded room and motioned him over.

The sharp crack of the billiard balls assaulted his ears, and by the time he reached his friend, his eyes were watering from the smoke. Maybe this wasn't such a good idea.

Jack introduced him to the men around his table, and they played a couple of games before Sam begged off.

"You should just see the little darling. I tell you she's a beauty and has a voice like an angel."

Sam turned as the voice reached his ears from the table next to them.

Laughter greeted the man's declaration. "Yeah, but I wouldn't be getting any ideas if I were you. They say she's a sweet young lady, but her father guards her with fists of steel."

Sam lifted his eyebrow and sent a puzzled glance at Jack.

"I think they're talking about the new singer at Harrigan's," Jack said. "Have you seen her yet?"

Sam shook his head. "I haven't been to a show in weeks."

"I hear there's a new musical comedy starting next Friday. Maybe the girls would enjoy it, and you could get a glimpse of the gorgeous Katherine O'Shannon." He laughed. "But don't fall for her and break Janet's heart. Sally would blame me."

"Don't worry. I hardly think Janet would care. We're only friends. And I'm not likely to fall for a showgirl. Even if I was so inclined, my folks would kill me."

"And if they didn't, I would. Couldn't stand by and watch you ruin your career." He slapped Sam on the shoulder. "So, shall I invite the girls for opening night?"

"Sure, sounds like fun. I'll stop by Sally's tomorrow after work and invite Janet. Shall we all ride over together?"

"No, let's go separately. I need to talk to Sally privately."

"Fine with me."

"Don't you want to know why?" Jack was grinning. In fact, it seemed like he'd been doing a lot of that tonight.

Jack glanced around, his face red with excitement. "I'm thinking about proposing marriage to Sally tonight."

Sam whistled and held his hand out to his beaming friend. "Congratulations!"

"If she says yes, you mean."

"She will. I'm sure of it."

"Maybe you'll be popping the question yourself soon. Janet's a lovely girl."

"Who just happens to be nothing more than a friend," Sam retorted. "Besides, marriage is the last thing on my mind."

But once more, the young woman from the Patch filled his head. He brushed the thought away and grabbed a billiard stick. "Come on. Maybe I'll let you win this one."

five

"How can I ever be thanking you for recommending me for this job, Katie? And me being nothing to you but a poor stranger."

Katie frowned at Bridget, who was pushing a moistened strand of thread through the tiny eye of her sewing needle.

"What do you mean 'nothing,' Bridget Thornton? You've become a dear friend to me, as I hope I have to you."

Bridget gasped. "And now I've gone and offended you. The one person, besides me ma, I have the most respect for."

Katie reached over and placed her hand momentarily on Bridget's arm. "Not at all. I just don't like to hear you belittling yourself. It hurts me."

"Then I won't be doing it again. I promise." The girl cast a shy smile at Katie then ducked her head over her work. "And Mr. Harrigan is a mighty good man to be paying for my room and board through the week. It'd be awfully hard to walk all the way here from the Patch and back again every day."

"Yes, it is nice of him to do that for the unmarried women of the cast."

"I thought Ma was going to stay on her knees all night, thanking the Lord for such a blessing. She said I should thank you and Mr. Harrigan for her, too. You can't imagine the difference my wages have made in our lives."

Katie thought she did know. The wonderful smell of stew now wafted through the Thornton home every day, and Mrs. Thornton and Bridget's little sister were both recovering, due to nourishment and the medicine Bridget had been able to provide. Katie and Bridget had become fast friends, and Katie had taken to dropping by to help with the endless mending when she wasn't rehearsing.

"Katie, I'm so excited you got the part. You must be about to burst with happiness."

Katie's heart thumped at the thought of her luck. It must be the Irish in her. Although, Grandmother had always reprimanded her whenever she'd said that. "Katherine, dear," she'd say with a worried little shake of her head, "blessings come from God. Not luck."

Katie shrugged. Whoever or whatever was responsible for her getting the part, she was thankful. If only some of those blessings would flow to the people of the Patch as well. "Bridget, what can we do to make things easier for your neighbors?"

"Why, I don't know, Katie. Most of the men are doing all they can. Wages are just so low. And most of the women have a passel of little ones to care for."

"Well, couldn't some sort of child care be arranged so that the women can bring in extra money?"

A little frown appeared on Bridget's face. "Some of the women do take turns, but it's not really enough to help. And when a woman has worked her own full shift, it's mighty hard to take a turn at running after someone else's brood."

Katie nodded, but wheels began to turn in her head. "What if. . ."

"What if what?"

"Nothing. Let me think on it a bit."

"Okay, but you'd better get onstage. I think it's almost time for you to rehearse."

"Oh my. You're right." Katie jumped up, tossed her mending in a basket, and throwing a hasty good-bye over her shoulder, headed out the door.

She arrived onstage just as Maggie was saying the opening lines. Her heart still thumped hard every time the moment for her one line drew near. But the rest of the cast assured her she was a natural and doing a wonderful job. Tomorrow was opening night, and Katie looked forward to the dress rehearsal and the party that would be held tonight.

After rehearsal, Katie and Bridget went back to Ma Casey's. The troupe was pretty rowdy with the excitement of the new show, so the two friends found a quiet place to talk out on the wide front porch.

"Okay, I have an idea," Katie said, leaning back in one of the wicker rockers.

"About what?"

"The children at the Patch."

"Hmm. I wouldn't be making decisions about other people's wee children. They won't be liking it."

Katie laughed. "No, no. They'll like this. It's to help the mothers who need to work. And it's only a suggestion."

"Well, in that case. . ."

"There's a society here in town that has established a day care for workers' children."

"We know about that. It's too far from the Patch to do any good. And I don't think the women there would trust outsiders to care for their children anyway."

"I know. But wouldn't it be possible to create something similar at Conley's Patch?"

"How would you be thinking we could bring that about?"

"Okay, first we'd need to find someone with a big enough house. Then several women can care for the children while the others work. The women who work could contribute a share of their earnings to pay the ones who care for the children. This way everyone is earning wages."

An expression of hope and excitement crossed Bridget's face. "It might work. But how do we get it started?"

"We could call a meeting for those who are interested in working. Once we introduce the plan, we can help them get organized. After that, it will be up to them to keep things going."

Excited, the girls discussed the possibility of the day care until Katie's father interrupted them. It was time for a light supper before dress rehearsal. They joined the rest of the troupe, then after supper, they headed for the theater.

Katie loved her costume. She was a little disappointed to find there was no wig with it, such as some of the others had. But Mr. Harrigan, laughing, assured her that her own bouncing golden curls were perfect for the part.

The celebration at Ma Casey's broke up early. Mr. Harrigan insisted. After all, he couldn't have a sleepy bunch of actors stumbling around the stage on opening day.

❧

"Oh, Sam, I'm so excited. I've never been to Harrigan's before."

Sam tried not to wince at the shrill tone of Janet's voice. Had she been this annoying before? And the way she clutched at his arm, digging her fingers into his flesh, made him wonder if she truly understood the nature of their friendship after all. The *clip-clop* of the horses' hooves seemed to be attempting to compete with the young woman's incessant chatter. But perhaps she was nervous. Forcing a smile, he turned to her. "Then I'm delighted to be the one to give you the pleasure."

She flashed a coquettish smile at him, and dropping her lashes, she turned away. "Oh, look! There are Jack and Sally."

The couple stood by the theater entrance, apparently awaiting Sam and Janet's arrival.

Sam pulled to a stop in front of Harrigan's and, after helping Janet from the carriage, threw a coin to a boy who, with obvious experience, grabbed the reins and led the horse and carriage away.

Janet joined Jack and Sally while Sam went to purchase their tickets.

Animated voices greeted them as they walked into the auditorium. They found their seats, very near the front, and Jack and Sally scooted in first.

As Sam seated himself on the aisle seat, the lights dimmed and the auditorium quieted.

The boisterous emcee greeted the audience and told a couple of jokes. Then he announced Katherine O'Shannon.

Sam glanced with curiosity toward the wings as a small figure walked out onstage. His breath caught, and he blinked. Surely it was his imagination. After all, the light was dim.

Then she stepped into the spotlight, and there was no doubt. That lovely smile. The golden curls. The sky blue eyes. Oh yes. It was her.

Sam sat mesmerized as she sang a pretty Irish ballad, turning it into a masterpiece, then stood to his feet and applauded loudly as she left the stage.

"Sam, you idiot, sit down."

Jack's whisper brought Sam back to his senses, and he realized he was the only one standing. He dropped back onto his chair but continued to applaud. After all, everyone else was clapping, too.

The girl walked back onto the stage and did a short encore, then she hurried off the stage.

As the emcee returned to the stage to announce the first act, Sam leaned back, suddenly conscience of the girl seated next to him. He glanced at her and was met with a look of fury and stony silence.

The curtain rose and the play began.

In the middle of the first act, Sam was delighted to see Katherine O'Shannon step onto the stage in a housemaid's uniform. After that, although she only appeared once more and spoke only one line, he had no idea what the rest of the play was about.

During intermission, Sam followed the other three to the lobby.

After the girls excused themselves, Jack turned to Sam with a look of unbelief. "Are you crazy? Why were you gaping at that actress? You'll be lucky if Janet ever speaks to you again, much less agrees to see you."

"It's her, Jack." Sam almost whispered the words.

"What? Who?"

"It's the girl from the train station," Sam said.

Suddenly, understanding appeared on Jack's face, and he frowned. "The one who lives at the Patch?"

"The very same."

Jack groaned. "Don't do something stupid, Sam. You'll regret it when you come to your senses."

Sam was saved from answering by the return of the girls.

Janet gave him a cold smile but took his arm as they returned to their seats to await the next act. "What do you think of actresses, Sally?" Janet turned to her cousin, but her words reached Sam clearly.

"Why, what do you mean?" Sally asked.

"Well, I've always heard their morals are atrocious. Haven't you heard that?" Without waiting for Sally to reply, Janet's malicious words continued. "Take that singer, for instance. She looks so demure, and her voice is so, so sweet. But of course, that's only an act. I wouldn't want to even think what sort of life she lives after the curtain goes down."

Jack and Sally stared at her in surprise, but Sam, attempting to hold back his anger, knew her words were spoken for his benefit. "Perhaps you should reserve your judgment. Especially about a girl you don't know." Sam heard the words almost before he realized he'd spoken.

Janet's mouth flew open in disbelief. "Well! If that's the sort of girl who interests you, I'm certainly glad I found out now." Her face was red, and she spoke loudly enough that people around them were taking notice.

Sam groaned inwardly. His parents would have been mortified if they'd heard him. "Janet, I apologize. I shouldn't have spoken to you as I did. It was ungentlemanly of me. But I do think you spoke those unkind words without thinking."

At her angry gasp, he realized he'd done it again. Well, he'd tried. At first.

"Well, the very idea! I refuse to stay in your presence any

longer. I'm leaving." The girl jumped up and, with Sam, Sally, and Jack trailing after, rushed to the lobby.

"I'll take you home then." He didn't want to miss another possible glimpse of Katherine, but he obviously couldn't let Janet leave unescorted.

"No, you most certainly will not take me home! I wouldn't go anywhere with you if I had to walk every step of the way home." She frowned at him and then turned her back. "But I'm sure Jack will see that I don't have to do that. After all, he is a gentleman."

"Sally and I will see you home, Janet, of course." He shook his head at Sam. "To be honest, I don't care for the show that much, and Sally and I have plans for the rest of the evening."

After they'd left, Sam headed back to his seat, feeling guilty. . .at first. He should probably have tried harder to reason with Janet. He couldn't really blame her for being angry. But then, he'd only been defending the honor of another young woman. Janet's words had been downright mean.

After a while, he managed to convince himself he'd done all he could and admitted he was relieved she'd left. Because he had no intention of leaving the theater without an attempt to speak to Katherine O'Shannon.

six

Katie bit her upper lip and squinted her eyes in an attempt to hold back the tears. She ran into the ladies' dressing room and flung herself onto a stool, her head leaning on the dressing table. The memory of the young man's shocked expression as he stared at her from the audience stabbed her, and humiliation tore at her in relentless frenzy.

"Katie! Whatever is the matter?" Fear sharpened Bridget's voice. "Did something go wrong onstage?"

Katie looked up. "No, no. It's nothing. Nothing at all. Just nerves, I guess." She stiffened and swiped at the moisture in her eyes. What right did he have to be shocked that she was an actress? He was probably some rich man's son who'd never worked a day in his life. The snob.

The other actresses spilled into the room, their sudden entrance catching Katie by surprise.

"What a great first night. I don't think we've had this good an opening since last holiday season." Caitlyn Brown threw her wig on a table and slipped off her shoes. "And Katie, honey, you did a wonderful job. Congratulations."

"Thank you." Furtively, Katie dabbed at her eyes.

A tap sounded on the door, and Caitlyn walked over and flung it open.

Katie gasped at the sight of her tormenter, holding a bouquet of flowers he must have bought from the street vendor outside the theater.

He cleared his throat, his clean-shaven face red with embarrassment. "Uh, could I speak with Miss O'Shannon?"

Caitlyn eyed him then glanced sideways at Katie, who shook her head. "Sorry. Miss O'Shannon is indisposed at the moment."

"Oh." He glanced across at Katie then looked away.

"But perhaps if you come back in ten minutes, she will see you."

His face brightened. "Good. Will you give her these?"

Caitlyn took the bouquet and shut the door. With a teasing look, she handed the flowers to Katie. "Your first performance and already an admirer at the door."

"Why did you tell him to come back?"

"Because he's a bonnie handsome lad and I couldn't resist the pleading in his eyes."

Katie removed her makeup and changed into her street clothes. Maybe she had misunderstood the look on his face. Perhaps it wasn't revulsion, after all.

Ten minutes later, right on schedule, another tap sounded on the door. She threw a reproachful look at Caitlyn and went to answer. She supposed she mustn't be rude.

He stood, hat in hand, and in spite of herself, she nearly melted at his smile.

"Miss O'Shannon?"

"Yes." She stepped out into the hall and closed the door. "Is there something I can do for you, sir?"

"You do remember me, don't you?"

"Of course. You're the gentleman who returned the napkin that fell off my basket." She paused then continued. "The man at the station."

He grinned and gave a little laugh. "Good. I was afraid you'd forgotten me."

"Sir, you know my name, but I have no idea of yours." She crossed her arms and waited, determined not to be at that sort of disadvantage another moment.

"Oh, I'm so sorry. I'm Sam Nelson."

She held out her hand for a shake, and to her surprise, he lifted it and brushed his lips softly against her fingers. A bolt went through her, and she jerked her hand away.

"Forgive me. I don't know what I was thinking." He smiled.

She shook her head and laughed. "Well, all right. You're forgiven. But don't ever take such liberties again." She tucked her hand into her pocket to make sure. "The flowers are lovely. Thank you."

"You're very welcome." He cleared his throat. "I wonder if you would consent to dine with me."

She drew back in surprise. "Tonight?"

"No, no. Of course not. How stupid of me. I'm sure you have plans. Well, how about tomorrow night?"

Katie blushed. She had no plans except to go home and get a good night's sleep. But she would never accept a dinner invitation on such short notice, especially from a young man she barely knew. Besides, her father had forbidden it. "No, I'm sorry. That won't be possible." She noticed she was picking at a nonexistent thread on her dress. She curled her fingers up and crammed her hand back into her pocket.

"I see. Very well, I'll see you tomorrow night. Thank you for allowing me to speak with you." He bowed, turned, and walked away.

What did he mean he'd see her tomorrow night? Didn't he hear her refuse his dinner invitation?

She turned and went inside, nearly knocking Caitlyn down. "Oh. You were listening!" Katie declared, scandalized.

Caitlyn burst out laughing. "Yes, I admit it. Unfortunately, I didn't hear much. Do tell us."

"There's nothing to tell. He invited me to dinner, and I refused. That's all."

"You refused? Why? He's gorgeous." Caitlyn rolled her eyes.

"Now you be leaving her alone." Bridget glared at the teasing actress. "Pay her no mind, Katie."

"Thanks, I won't." She smiled at her defender and at the playful actress, happy to have friends who cared.

Katie and Bridget walked home. As they trailed behind her father and Rosie, Katie told her friend about the incident at the station and the encounter at Conley's Patch.

A thoughtful expression settled across Bridget's brow. "It seems to me he's setting his cap for you. Be careful. Who knows if his intentions are honorable or not?"

Fear shot through Katie. Could Bridget be right? It was strange that he'd had that shocked look on his face. Then he came with flowers and an invitation so soon.

Katie gasped. Did Sam Nelson think she was a loose woman?

❧

Sam reached inside his vest pocket and pulled out the string of tickets he'd purchased before he'd gone backstage. Row one, center seat. If the show outlasted what he'd bought, he'd buy more.

He placed the tickets in the top drawer of his bedside table and berated himself for being so bold with Miss O'Shannon. Just because he'd been thinking of her for weeks, did he think she would jump into his arms?

Sam's thoughts continued to chastise him as he tossed and turned in his bed, finally falling into a troubled sleep sometime near dawn.

He was front and center the following night. Once more he carried a bouquet to her dressing room and asked her to dine with him the next evening. She declined the invitation.

There was no show the next day, as the theater was closed on Sundays, and Sam spent the afternoon fidgeting until his mother finally turned to him with a frown.

"What in the world is the matter with you, Sam?"

"I'm fine." He sent her a rather sick smile that even he knew was unconvincing.

Suddenly her face brightened. "You're in love, aren't you? That's why you're mooning around."

"Really, Mother. I'm not some young lad with a crush."

"Mmm-hmm." She busied herself with her knitting. "Who is she?"

Sam was silent for a moment as his mind considered

opening up to his mother about Katherine O'Shannon. No, not yet. He didn't need a reaction from her just yet. "Mother, when there is actually a young woman in my life, I promise to tell you all about her." There. Not a lie. But maybe not the complete truth either.

The two weeks that followed were a world of contradictions. During the day, Sam was the serious, hardworking attorney, focusing his attention on the Flannigan case.

Evenings were a different matter altogether. Like a lovesick schoolboy, in the middle seat of the first row, he sat mesmerized by Katherine O'Shannon.

Every night, after being turned down again, he told himself he would stay away from Harrigan's from now on. But the following night, there he sat, swimming in the depths of her blue eyes. If his mother had again accused him of being in love, he couldn't have denied it.

Jack was about to lose patience with him. "Sam, my friend, you're going to let that showgirl rob you of your partnership."

"No, I'm not. And don't call her 'that showgirl' in that tone of voice."

His friend sighed. "Sorry, but man, you're losing your mind."

Sam bristled. "I'm doing my work just fine."

The Flannigan folder peeked out from under the stack of books piled on Sam's desk. Something about the case still bothered him. At this point, he was mostly getting paperwork together and checking for any evidence that might have been overlooked.

Making a sudden decision, Sam stood up. "As a matter of fact, I'm heading out to Conley's Patch now to interview Flannigan again. I've got a hunch there's something I'm missing."

"The Patch, huh?" Jack's suspicious tone grated on Sam. "You sure you're not hoping to run into the actress?"

"I hope I do, but that's not my reason for going. I honestly do have business to attend to."

"All right. But I hope you know what you're doing."

Sam considered his friend's words all the way to Conley's Patch.

The heat in the Patch radiated from the stinking street, and the smell from the ditch running down the center was so bad Sam would have covered his nose and mouth with a handkerchief, but he didn't want to offend Flannigan more than he already had.

The meeting with Flannigan did little except confuse Sam. The injured man's attitude and demeanor simply didn't line up with the accusations against him.

Disturbed, he left the house, determined not to let the seeming inconsistencies get him off course. Flannigan should probably be performing at Harrigan's. After all, a con man wouldn't get very far if he wasn't convincing.

He got into his buggy and headed back to the office.

A young woman walked down the dirty street, her golden curls peeking out from beneath her bonnet. The tilt of her head, the set of her shoulders, even from the back he knew it was her. He urged the horse forward and pulled up beside her. "Miss O'Shannon."

Startled, she turned. Her eyes grew wide, and Sam knew he wasn't mistaking the gladness he saw there.

"May I give you a lift somewhere? It's awfully hot to be walking."

Nervously, she glanced around. "I had hoped to hail a cabbie, but there doesn't seem to be one in sight."

He didn't want to say that cabbies didn't usually hang around this area. Strange she didn't know that. He stepped out of the carriage. "I assure you, I only wish to help you if you'll allow it."

Her eyes shifted with uncertainty then looked fully into his own, nearly robbing him of the ability to breathe. "If it's not an inconvenience," she said in a tiny voice. "I could use a ride to the theater." The feel of her tiny gloved hand filled him with awe as he helped her into the carriage.

He urged the horse to a trot and glanced at her with a smile.

A pink blush washed over her face, and she gave him a sweet smile. "Mr. Nelson, I feel I should explain why I haven't accepted any of your invitations when you've been so kind." She gave a slight cough.

"You owe me no explanation, Miss O'Shannon. You have a right to refuse me if you please."

"But you see, I would have accepted if it were up to me." Once more the pretty blush caressed her cheeks.

"What do you mean?" He hoped his eagerness didn't startle her.

"My father has forbidden me to accept invitations from any young man without his approval. And after all, he doesn't even know you."

Sam tried hard to control the grin that started in his heart and worked its way to his lips. But it was a hopeless task. "Well," he said, "we'll just have to do something about that, won't we?"

seven

Katie jumped out of the carriage before the young man had a chance to assist her. If her father saw her, there was no telling what he'd do. Oh, why hadn't she asked Mr. Nelson to drop her off a block away from the theater?

She heard his startled exclamation as her feet hit the street, and she turned, throwing him an apologetic look. "Thank you so much for the ride. It was very kind of you, but I must be going."

She started off toward the side of the building, hoping to avoid anyone she knew. At the sight of Bobby and Molly standing at the corner, she groaned and stopped.

Bobby shot a glare at Mr. Nelson, who still sat in his carriage, watching her. "Who's that?" Bobby demanded, sending Katie a reproachful look.

"Why, he's an acquaintance of mine, Bobby Brown, if it's any of your business." She frowned at him, and he turned and stalked off.

"Ah, poor, poor Bobby. Now you've gone and broken his heart." Molly grinned and looked pointedly at the carriage and its occupant.

Katie felt heat rise to her face. Why in the world was he still sitting there? "Well, I don't know how his heart could be broken," Katie retorted. "I've never given him reason to think I was interested in anything but friendship." Well, maybe she had flirted a little bit. A pang of conscience stabbed her as she remembered her ploy to get information from him about Conley's Patch.

"If you say so, dear." Molly rounded the corner of the building.

Katie's heart thumped. She didn't need to look back to know he was still there, watching her. But she looked anyway. Land's sake. What was he doing?

He tipped his hat and grinned.

Katie waved and then bolted around the corner, her stomach doing little flips. Stepping through the open door into the theater, she couldn't help the smile that tilted her lips.

"I saw that." Molly was waiting for her just inside the door.

Setting her chin, Katie sent Molly what she hoped was a firm look. "Mr. Nelson is merely an acquaintance. Not even a friend, much less a suitor."

Molly laughed. "Hey, I'm only fooling. Don't get riled up, now."

In the crowded dressing room, Katie made her way past women getting ready for the afternoon performances. She hurried to get into her costume then sat at a dressing table to apply her makeup.

Oh, what had she done? She knew better than to accept a ride from a man who was practically a stranger. When her father found out, and he would, he'd likely put her on the first train back to the farm. Katie cringed at the thought. But there was no getting around it. She had to tell him herself. Right after the show.

For the first time, she didn't enjoy performing. Her heart didn't soar as it usually did when she sang her solo, and she recited her lines without feeling. As soon as she'd made her final exit, she rushed to the dressing room and poured her heart out to Bridget.

"Now, now. Don't be frettin' so. After all, your da would probably rather you took the ride than be walking down the streets of the Patch. What with all the—" The girl stopped and gave Katie a curious look. "What do you think a fine young gentleman would be doing at Conley's Patch?"

"Well, I don't know. Maybe he had business there." She frowned. What was Bridget getting at?

"At the Patch? What sort of business would he be in?"

"I'm sure I don't know. How should I?"

"If he's going to be hanging around you, you'd best be finding out everything you can about him. Including his business." Bridget's eyes widened. "He could be a gambler or even criminal of some sort. They often look like gentlemen."

"Bridget, you're scaring me."

"Well, and I mean to. A girl can't be too careful, after all."

Katie sighed. "Guess I needn't worry about it. If my father doesn't send me away, he'll watch me like a hawk."

"I won't be arguing with you about that." Bridget darted a sympathetic look at her.

Just then, the rest of the women flocked into the room, and Katie took a deep breath. The show was over. There was no putting it off any longer.

She found her father removing the paint from his face.

"Katie, my girl." He sprang from the chair and planted a kiss on her cheek. "It's glad I am you came to see me. You're usually running off someplace before I can hardly say hello and good-bye."

"You're stretching the truth, Pa, and well you know it." Katie smiled, relieved to find him in a good mood. Maybe he wouldn't be so angry after all.

"Pa, there's something I need to tell you." She cleared her throat and swallowed.

"Well, and here I am. What is it?"

"Please don't be angry with me, because I'm very sorry."

He frowned and peered at her. "Have you been spending too much of me hard-earned money now? Is that it?"

She shook her head vehemently. "I have my own money now." The very idea.

"That hasn't been stopping you from spending mine, too, now, has it?" He patted her on the arm. "But I don't mind a bit, my Katie girl. So don't be fretting."

Maybe she should let well enough alone. After all, there was no harm done. She gave her father a tremulous smile and turned to go. No, it would be much worse if he found out from someone else. She turned and faced him again. "I accepted a ride to the theater from a young man this afternoon."

"Ah yes. You'll be referring to Mr. Nelson. I thanked him nicely for rescuing my daughter from the streets of shantytown." He pursed his lips and scowled. "And how many times have I told you not to be walking around Conley's Patch by yourself?"

Katie gasped. He told her father? But how was that possible? "When did he tell you?"

"Right after he dropped you off at the door. He wanted me to know why you were in his carriage. A fine upstanding young lawyer, he is. And very concerned that I might get the wrong idea."

Gladness and relief rose up in Katie's heart. An attorney. Good. So he wasn't a criminal, after all. "And you don't mind that I accepted a ride from him?"

"Not after he explained that he was a patron of Harrigan's and recognized you from your performance." He glared at her again. "He was concerned you might be accosted. Otherwise, such a fine young gentleman would have never suggested such a thing."

ie

Sam whistled through the grin that wouldn't leave his face as he walked into the office. Michael O'Shannon was a good man and a grateful father.

It had been obvious Katie hadn't wanted to be seen in his carriage. When he saw her talking to a couple of performers outside the theater, he knew he had to avert scandal. And perhaps get on her father's good side at the same time. It had been a streak of genius that led him to reveal to Katie's father that he'd given her a lift. Instead of being angry at his daughter and thinking the worst of Sam, he had slapped Sam on the back and thanked him for taking care of Katie.

Now, if Sam could only be patient and let O'Shannon get

to know him better, he thought he had a pretty good chance of winning the protective father over so he could court his daughter.

Charlie Jenkins looked up from his desk and gave him a nod. "Glad to see you in a good mood, sir. Your father wants to see you. He said as soon as you got here."

"Uh-oh. Is it bad?"

Charlie glanced around and lowered his voice. "I wouldn't want to say, Mr. Nelson, but I will say he didn't seem very happy."

"Well, nothing is going to spoil my mood." Sam headed to his father's office, wondering what he'd done. "Charlie said you wanted to see me."

The senior Mr. Nelson turned slowly and peered at Sam through narrowed eyes. "Jeremiah Howard, *your client,* waited for you for some time. Would you mind divulging where you've spent your afternoon?"

Sam looked at his father in surprise. "I don't remember an appointment with Howard."

"That's beside the point. If you'd been in the office, he could have spoken to you instead of railing at me for two hours."

"I went to see Flannigan again. Something just isn't ringing true to me." He picked up a newspaper from his father's desk and riffled through it.

"So, did you get anything out of the man?"

Sam continued to scan the newspaper, wondering what to say. "Father, Chauncey Flannigan doesn't seem like a con man to me."

When his father didn't say anything, Sam looked up and met silence.

Eugene Nelson eyed his son. "Don't forget who our client is, Samuel."

"I won't. I promise."

"Very well. Send a messenger boy to Howard's office with an appointment for tomorrow."

"I will, sir."

Sam dispatched the messenger then sat at his desk, tapping his fingers against the oak desktop. His father was right. Whatever he personally thought about Howard, he was representing the man and needed to give him his best. He'd been meaning to visit the lumberyard and speak to some of the employees and decided that would be the first thing on his agenda in the morning. While he was there, he'd try to meet the foreman who'd been on duty that day.

Sam leaned back and considered what else could be accomplished while he was in the area. The two tavern witnesses who'd given statements needed to be spoken to. It wouldn't do for them to waver in their accounts of the fight.

Taking a legal pad from his desk drawer, Sam made a list of questions for the men he hoped to interview. He also intended to look over conditions at the lumber mill and make sure there was nothing to which an accusing finger could be pointed.

The shuffling of feet and opening and closing of file cabinets announced the office was getting ready to close for the day.

Cramming his pad into his briefcase, Sam stood and made his way to the front, amid friendly good-byes. The thought of seeing Katherine quickened his steps. He was relieved to see that Charlie had sent someone to the livery to bring his horse and carriage around.

As he rode home in the stifling heat, he glanced up, hoping for the sight of a rain cloud. It was the middle of September. But the driest September Sam could remember.

When he arrived at home, he found his mother in the kitchen supervising dinner preparations.

"Sam, dear. We're having guests for dinner. Could you possibly bring the ice cream freezer out? Everything is mixed and ready to go. You have time to crank out a batch before you change, if you wouldn't mind."

"Of course, Mother. Let me go hang up my suit coat." When he came back downstairs, he went to the storage room off the kitchen and took his mother's pride and joy out of its box.

She poured the mixture of cream, sugar, and vanilla into the container and added salt and cracked ice to the freezer.

Sam started cranking. "Who are the guests, Mother?"

"Oh, I think you'll be pleasantly surprised. The Langleys' niece, Martha, is visiting, and Ella wants her to meet young people her own age. I told her I was certain you would be happy to meet Martha and perhaps introduce her to some of your friends."

Sam grinned, amused at another of his mother's attempts to help him find her future daughter-in-law. She'd been hinting for some time that he should be settling down. She'd be quite surprised if she knew he had already chosen his future bride. "Yes, of course, Mother. I'd be happy to show her around, but I have plans for tonight."

She held both hands up to her pretty, plump face. "Oh dear. I should have checked with you first. But I'm sure they'll be leaving by nine. Would that upset your plans? I'll be so embarrassed if you can't be here."

When Sam saw his mother's hopeful expression, he knew he wouldn't be seeing Katherine O'Shannon tonight.

eight

Katie walked into the stifling room and held her breath, trying not to gag from the smell of cabbage and onions steaming from a pot on top of the small stove in the corner. The one-room, run-down shack contained two beds pushed up against opposite walls. A threadbare, faded quilt lay neatly folded at the end of each bed, and twin rickety chests stood side by side against the front wall. Four chairs, with sagging seats, hugged the uncovered table near the back door.

A colorful painting of an Irish meadow on the wall above the table, the only suggestion of color or beauty in the neat but drab room, caught Katie by surprise. As she followed Bridget and her mother, she noticed the dirt floor was swept clean and smooth. Mrs. Thornton opened the back door, and Katie sighed with relief as they walked out into the small backyard and she inhaled fresh air.

About a dozen women stood in clusters of twos and threes, seeming to ignore the nearby hodgepodge of chairs, stools, and wooden barrels.

A tiny woman, her blue eyes sparkling and black hair pulled back in a bun, turned from two others and hurried over to Mrs. Thornton. "How are ya farin', Margaret? I hope this heat won't be too much for ya."

"I'm feeling much better. Thank ya, Susan." The paleness of her lips and dark circles beneath her warm brown eyes belied the brave words, but her neighbor nodded and smiled.

"It's glad I am to be hearing it." She turned to Bridget and patted her on the shoulder. "And here you are working and helping your ma and the wee little one. A good thing."

"Mrs. Bailey," Bridget said, taking Katie's hand, "I'd like for you to meet my friend Katie O'Shannon."

The woman smiled. "It's pleased I am to meet you, Miss O'Shannon. And happy that you'd be caring about the poor people of Conley's Patch."

Katie blushed. "Please call me Katie, ma'am. And really, it's just an idea for child care that Bridget and I came up with."

"Well, anything to help put food in the mouths of the children is a good idea."

Mrs. Thornton shook her head, a worried look on her face. "I'm not sure everyone is agreein' with you."

"Well, and if they're not, they should be. Now you be sittin' down and resting yourselves."

Katie felt a glow of pride as she sat on a stool next to Bridget. Finally, someone older was taking her seriously.

The other women gathered around and found seats then looked expectantly at Katie. Her hands sweaty and breath coming in gulps, she threw a frantic glance at Bridget. Maybe this wasn't such a good idea after all.

Bridget stood and smiled at her friends and neighbors. "I'd like ya all to meet my friend Katie O'Shannon. She's the one who helped me get my job at Harrigan's."

"And proud we are of you, Bridget, dear." The gray-haired woman smiled sweetly at Bridget.

"Sure and it's a shame on you, Granny Laurie, if you're proud of one of our own lasses a-workin' in a devil's den of iniquity." A woman, just entering the Bailey yard, flashed a hard look at Katie. "And you a-prancin' around here callin' yourself Irish and pretending you want to help us."

Katie gasped. Had she heard the woman right? Surely not. Most of the ladies were frowning at the woman who'd spoken, but she noticed two or three nodding in agreement.

Mrs. Bailey stood. "The shame is on you, Bridie McDermott, for insulting a kind young stranger in our midst, as well as our own Bridget Thornton."

Katie stood. "Maybe we should leave, Bridget," she whispered.

"No." Bridget grabbed Katie's arm and tugged her back to her seat. "We're not going to let that woman and her bitterness keep us from doing what we came to do."

Katie, surprised at Bridget's assertiveness, acquiesced.

"I hope you'll stay and listen to what these young girls have to say, Bridie," Mrs. Bailey continued. "But if you're only here to cause trouble, you can be leaving."

One of the women who'd seemed to agree with Bridie motioned her over to a chair next to her. With a venomous look at Katie, the angry woman walked over and sat down.

Somehow Katie managed to get through the meeting, letting Bridget do most of the talking. Bridie McDermott was right. Who was she to think she could help these women? Just because she saw a need and felt compassion didn't mean she could do anything about the problem.

Shame washed over her. She'd been proud to think they'd listen to her and thank her and tell her how wonderful she was. She saw that now. Humiliation pounded at her temples, and by the time the meeting ended and she and Bridget left, she had a full-blown headache.

"Katie, they loved the idea of the day care. Did you hear the excitement in their voices?"

Katie stared at her friend, who continued to chatter. "Are you sure?"

"Of course I'm sure. And where were you that you didn't see it, too?"

Throwing her friend a sheepish grin, Katie said, "I guess I was thinking about what a failure I was."

"Ah, Katie. But this isn't about you now, is it?" Bridget ducked her head. "I'm sorry. I need to be buttoning my lips."

"No. You're right. This isn't about me. It's about the people of Conley's Patch. Your people, Bridget. And if any credit is due, it's to you, not me."

"Not me, neither. The credit goes to God. Only God."

The girls climbed into Harrigan's carriage, and the driver

clicked to the horse. As they rode in silence to Ma Casey's, Katie thought about her friend's words. So much like Grandmother's. She hadn't thought much about God since the day she boarded the train for Chicago. When she did think of Him, it was as though He were some unreachable, powerful Being, watching over His world from afar. Did God really intervene in the daily worries of ordinary people?

She didn't remember Him ever intervening in hers.

❧

Sam stood in the corridor outside Michael O'Shannon's dressing room, his heart thumping, waiting for a reaction from Michael O'Shannon. . .any reaction.

The man merely stood there, a grim expression on his face, peering at Sam. "So you're wanting to court my daughter, are ye?"

"Yes, sir. With your permission, of course." Sam waited again as Katie's father bit his bottom lip and looked up at the ceiling.

"Well," O'Shannon said, "it's like this, Nelson. I'm inclined to like you, and it's true I'm beholden to you for escorting my little girl away from the Patch. But before I'll be letting you court her, I'll be getting to know you better."

"I understand, sir." Inwardly, Sam groaned. How long would it take O'Shannon to think he knew him well enough?

"So, with that in mind, I'll be expecting you for dinner on Sunday." He motioned with his hand, and Sam followed him into the men's dressing room where he wrote on a small card. "Here's the address. We sit down to table at three on Sundays, and Ma Casey frowns on anyone being late."

Sam stuck the card in his inside jacket pocket and held out his hand to O'Shannon. "Thank you, sir. I won't be late."

He checked his pocket watch. Almost time for the evening performance, and he didn't want to miss Katie's solo. He dashed to his seat, unable to help the bounce in his step as he walked down the aisle. He'd half expected O'Shannon to give him a kick in the pants and throw him out of the theater.

Programs rustled all around as Katie walked, smiling, onto the stage. He fought the urge to stand to his feet and shush them all.

Sam caught his breath as she looked straight at him. He smiled, and she blushed and lowered her eyes. Pride arose in Sam as Katie began to sing. Her sweet ballad moved the audience to tears. His girl. His girl, Katie. Well, she would be, if he had a say in it. He'd move the ocean if he had to, because he was in love with the girl. There was no denying it, even to himself.

After the performance, he rushed backstage and tapped on the door. This time, Katie herself opened it. He complimented her on her performance, gave her a wink and a lingering glance, then tipped his hat and left. He didn't want to take a chance on angering her father. He hoped to have a long talk with her after dinner Sunday.

As his horse trudged toward home, Sam leaned back in the buggy and wiped his linen handkerchief across his brow. For so late at night, the temperature didn't seem to have cooled off much, if any at all.

The heat hit him as he walked into the house, although it seemed every window was open. He went into the parlor where his mother sat on the flowered cushions of a Chippendale settee, fanning herself.

"Hello, Mother." He leaned over to kiss her cheek.

"Oh, Sam. I can't believe this weather."

"I know. I'm sure you're uncomfortable." He sat in a wing-backed chair near her.

"Yes, I am." She held up the newspaper she'd been reading. "Did you know we've only had an inch and a half of rain since the Fourth of July?"

Sam nodded. "It's terribly dry."

"Yes. The autumn leaves won't be pretty at all this year."

"I know you'll be disappointed." She looked forward each

year to the changing of summer into autumn.

"Yes, but at least we have our home." She breathed a soft sigh. "Thank the Lord for that."

"Harrumph." Sam looked up to see his father standing in the doorway.

"Hello, Father."

"Well, son, how was your evening?"

"Enjoyable. Thank you for asking."

"Hmm, out to dinner with friends, I suppose?"

"Actually, I went to the theater," Sam said briefly. He grinned as his mother perked up.

"Oh, how nice, dear. Did you take a young lady with you?"

"No, as a matter of fact, I went alone."

"Oh. Which theater?"

"Harrigan's." Sam held his breath, afraid of what was coming. He should have been more careful.

His father was the one who responded. "Hmm. Haven't you been going to Harrigan's a lot lately?"

"Well, I don't know if I'd say a lot."

"I believe they've been running the same show for several weeks, haven't they?" His father's knowing glance seemed to bore into Sam.

Sam fixed his gaze on a vase of flowers standing on the rosewood table in the corner. Anything to avoid his father's intense scrutiny.

"I believe so." Once more he avoided his father's stare.

His father turned his gaze on Sam's mother. "Amy, I'm going on the porch to smoke. Why don't you go up and change into something cooler. I'll be up shortly."

"Very well, Eugene." She arose and sauntered from the room.

"This blasted heat is getting to her. I'm not sure how much longer she can stand it."

Sam looked at his father in surprise. "Oh, but surely she'll be fine."

"Yes, yes. I'm sure you're right." He opened the front door and stepped out onto the porch, with Sam close behind.

They stood in silence for a moment, listening to the chorus of crickets and night birds.

"All right, Sam. Out with it. Why are you spending so much time at Harrigan's?"

Sam took a deep breath. How could he answer truthfully without revealing too much? He knew his parents wouldn't approve. After all, they didn't know Katie. They'd assume the worst. "I enjoy the Irish troupe, Father. And the show is hilarious. I've had so much on my mind lately with the Flannigan case that I needed a diversion."

The keen look his father shot at him said he didn't believe a word of it. "And this diversion. . .it wouldn't happen to wear skirts, would it, son?"

Sam could feel the heat in his face. He coughed. "Father, I've had a busy day. I'm going up to bed. Perhaps we can discuss this another time."

"But—"

"Good night, Father."

Sam went up to his room. He removed his coat and flung it across a chair. A tiny white card fell out onto the floor. Katie's address. Sam picked it up and scanned the contents.

Ma Casey's Boardinghouse. Sam peered at the address scratched below. It was near the downtown area. Katie didn't live at the Patch? Relief washed over him. But why in the world was she spending so much time in that dangerous shantytown?

nine

Katie sat beside Sam on the porch steps, with the door open for propriety. A haze blanketed the moonlight, and even the gaslight on the corner was almost useless, veiled as it was by the smoke that hung over the city. Her father had given tentative permission last week for Sam to court her. He'd even allowed them to go for walks without a chaperone but only in the daytime.

"A penny for your thoughts, Miss O'Shannon."

Katie knew it was respect that kept him from using her first name. But to be honest, she was getting a bit impatient with his continued use of "Miss." How awkward would it be to be kissed by someone who addressed her so formally? She blushed at the direction of her thoughts. The very idea. As if she'd allow him to kiss her.

Katie cleared her throat. "I was thinking about the terrible fires across the river." Well, she couldn't very well tell him what she'd really been thinking.

"Yes, terrible. I hope they get them under control before the wind changes."

Katie tensed, wishing she'd thought up a different lie. The possibility of the warehouses along the river catching fire was too frightening to talk about.

"Miss O'Shannon. . ."

"Oh, for heaven's sake, call me Katie." At his silence, she turned her head to look at him. When her eyes met his, her stomach sank. His usual smile and that crinkle in his eyes were gone. Had she offended him? Oh, when would she learn to button her lip? "I'm so sorry," she whispered. "I don't know what you must think of me."

The muscles in his face relaxed, and relief shot through Katie as he smiled. "I think you're perfectly wonderful. And if you're certain you won't think I'm being disrespectful, I'd be delighted to call you Katie."

"Of course I won't. After all, it is my name."

"Very well then, Katie it is. And it would be my pleasure if you'd call me Sam."

Katie had been calling him Sam in her mind since she'd heard his name, but of course he didn't know that. "All right. Sam." There. A little bubble rose up in her stomach. Almost like a giggle, only inside. She pressed her lips together and tried unsuccessfully to prevent the smile that tilted her lips. And then she said it again, "Sam."

He grinned, and the crinkle returned to his eyes. "Thank you."

The screen door opened behind them, and Katie's father stepped out on the porch. "Well now, daughter, it's about time you were coming inside. Morning comes early."

While Katie's father stood with lips pursed in a silent whistle, Sam said good night.

Katie watched him drive away then followed her father inside.

Bridget, who had spent the day at her mother's, sat in the parlor talking to Rosie. When she saw Katie, she stood. "I'm going to bed. Good night, everyone."

Katie stared after her friend. How strange. Bridget didn't even speak to her. Was she upset about something or perhaps coming down with a sickness?

Determined to get to the bottom of her friend's off behavior, Katie followed Bridget upstairs, catching her as she opened the door to her bedroom. "Bridget, wait."

The girl turned, a look of near panic on her face. Her attempt at a smile wouldn't have fooled a tot. "Yes, Katie?"

"What's wrong with you? You pushed right by me without so much as a glance."

"I'm sorry. I'm tired, and I guess I didn't see you."

"Of course you saw me," Katie retorted. "You can't pretend you didn't. Please tell me what's wrong. Have I somehow offended you?"

Bridget's face crumpled. "Won't ya come inside? There's something I need to be telling you."

Curious and a little uneasy, Katie stepped inside Bridget's tiny room.

"Here. You take the chair, and I'll sit on the end of the bed," Bridget said, still not looking at her.

Katie sat in the small cushioned rocking chair. "Now what is it?"

"I hate to be the one tellin' ya this. I know how much ya like the man, and I don't want to be losing your friendship."

"Bridget!" Katie stomped her foot against the hardwood floor. "Just get on with it. Nothing could break up our friendship."

Bridget continued to stare at her silently, and Katie began to fidget. Could it be that Bridget had feelings for Sam? Heat washed over her entire body.

"Has Mr. Nelson told you what his business is at Conley's Patch?"

Oh, a business matter. Relief welled up in her. "Well, no, the subject never came up. I suppose he has a client there. He's a lawyer, you know."

"A client?" A short, humorless laugh exploded from Bridget's mouth. "And who at the Patch do you think would have the money for a lawyer?"

"Perhaps he's doing volunteer work."

Bridget bit her lip and twisted her plain white handkerchief. "Have ya met my next-door neighbors, the Flannigans?"

"No, I don't think so."

"Chauncey Flannigan was severely injured while doing his job at a warehouse awhile back. He's been unable to work, plus he has doctor and hospital bills he can't afford to pay. His employer refused to give him any compensation at all, even denying that Chauncey was hurt there."

"Oh, I remember seeing Sam come from that house one day." Excitement raised Katie's voice. "So that explains it. Sam must be representing Mr. Flannigan without charge."

Bridget shook her head, and a vise seemed to clamp on to Katie's heart and squeeze. She wanted to put her hands over her ears. Shout at her friend to stop talking. Sam was a good man. She knew he was.

"I'm sorry, Katie. It's true Mr. Nelson is working on the case, but it's not Chauncey he's tryin' to help. He's working for Jeremiah Howard, the man who owns the warehouse."

Anger like fire shot through Katie. How could he? Here she was, trying to find a way to help the people at the Patch, and he was trying to push them down further. Didn't he believe in justice? He seemed so kind.

His arrogant look that day at the train station flashed through her mind. He hadn't been kind then. Of course, he'd apologized for his rudeness and explained the reason without trying to excuse his behavior. But perhaps that was because he was attracted to her. "I'm sure there must be a mistake, Bridget. I'll talk to him. But if he is indeed representing a cruel employer and refuses to listen to reason, I can assure you he won't be coming around here anymore."

❧

"Katie, you don't understand. The shanty Irish are a lazy bunch who'd rather lie, steal, and cheat than work." Sam had arrived a half hour ago, expecting a warm welcome from Katie. Her father had finally agreed to allow him to escort her to dinner unaccompanied. He'd been looking forward to it all day.

Her face had paled. "The Irish are lazy? And have you forgotten my father is Irish and I'm half Irish? Are you saying I'm lazy? That my pa is lazy? Why, he could outwork a soft-handed evil lawyer any time of the day."

Sam felt the blood leave his face. "No. Of course not. I didn't say all Irish are lazy. I'm talking about the shanty Irish."

"So you're only referring to folks like my best friend, Bridget." She blew a lock of golden hair from her eyes. Eyes that glared like a pair of torches.

"Katie, please be reasonable."

"Reasonable? And is it reasonable to peg a whole community of people as lazy thieves and liars? I'd like to know where you get your information, Sam Nelson. How dare you assume that all the men in Conley's Patch are lazy and shiftless. Aren't there shiftless, lazy men in your neighborhood? Well? Aren't there?"

Sam drew back. Oscar Willows who lived down the street from the Nelsons—as far as Sam knew, he'd never worked a day in his life. Lived off his mother's family inheritance and spent his days and nights gambling and drinking whiskey. But that had nothing to do with this. "I have witnesses who say Flannigan walked away from the warehouse on his own two feet with only minor injuries. I also have signed affidavits from two men who claim to have witnessed a tavern fight in which Flannigan was injured."

Katie placed her hands on her hips. "How very convenient for Jeremiah Howard. I wonder how much he's paying these so-called witnesses. Perhaps you'd better go find out, Mr. Nelson." Katie turned on her heel and walked inside, slamming the screen door behind her.

Sam slapped his hat against his leg and plopped it back on his head. With tight lips, he stalked off the porch and climbed into his buggy. Lost in his thoughts, he gave the horse its head and soon found himself near his own neighborhood. Not wishing to converse with anyone, he urged the horse around a corner, with a vague idea of finding someplace quiet to have dinner.

How could she be so unreasonable? She seemed to have

tunnel vision where the people of the Patch were concerned. Why was she so certain?

Once more, doubt wormed its way into his thoughts. Should he consider again the possibility that his father was wrong about the shanty Irish, and Flannigan in particular? Katie had been so angry and so sure of herself. Doubtless she knew something about the people of Conley's Patch. Sam was now aware of the charitable work she did there, as well as her desire to help the people, especially the children.

Deep in thought, he rode past the downtown district toward the river and soon found himself near Flannigan's neighborhood. As he drove aimlessly through the Patch, raucous curses and bawdy laughter assailed him from the darkness. After just coming off Michigan Avenue with its gaslights and brightly lit stores, an uneasiness shot through him. Perhaps this hadn't been the wisest course of action. The only lights, dim and flickering, came from the taverns lining the main street of Conley's Patch. He slapped his reins, wishing he'd had the forethought of switching the buggy for his horse, Jude.

As he rounded a corner onto a pitch black, narrow street, he heard scuffling and a sharp cry. Pulling his buggy to a halt, he peered into the darkness.

A pair of shadows hunched over a kneeling figure, pounding him with their fists. Sam jumped from the buggy and ran toward them. "Hey, you! What do you think you're doing?"

Before he could reach them, the two took off running toward the river.

The victim struggled to his feet and took the hand that Sam offered. "Thank ya."

"Are you injured?"

"Naw," the man panted, "just me pride, I guess."

"Were you robbed? Or did they just have a grudge against you?"

He stretched his back. "Oh, I was robbed, I was. Just comin' home with me pay. They took every cent. Took the bread from me children's mouths, they did."

"I have my buggy. I'll be glad to take you to find an officer of the law to report this."

A short laugh emitted from between the man's teeth. "Ain't no officers around here. Wouldn't be no use if there was. Me money's long gone now. Thanks for coming to my rescue. Name's Jack O'Hooley."

"Sam Nelson. I'm glad I was passing by." Sam reached into his coat pocket and pulled out some bills. "Here, buy some food for your family."

O'Hooley drew back with a scowl. "What do ye think I am? I ain't takin' no charity. A man takes care of his own." He turned and stalked off.

Sam stood staring at the money still in his hand. The fellow couldn't have much left, and he still refused the money.

O'Hooley stopped in front of a shack midway down the street and looked back. "I thank you again for your help and your good intentions. Don't worry none. We'll manage. We always do."

Stunned, Sam returned to his carriage. How could this happen to a peaceful family man walking home from work? It was almost as though the attackers had been waiting to accost their victim. Sam drove around the neighborhood, searching for a patrolman. He could at least report the incident.

Thirty minutes later, he pulled on the reins, bringing the carriage to a halt in front of a small café. Not one police officer in the whole neighborhood. Where in the world were they?

He tethered his horse and went inside. As he sat drinking a cup of coffee, he asked the man wiping the counter about the absence of patrolmen in the area.

With a laugh, the man continued wiping. "Are you nuts? They won't come down here at night. Can't say as I blame 'em. They're overworked and underpaid as it is. Why risk their lives in a place like this?"

Later, in the safety of his home, Sam couldn't fall asleep. Every time he shut his eyes, the face of the proud, hardworking O'Hooley, who'd been robbed of everything, hovered in his thoughts. That man was not shiftless or lazy. He was just a poorly paid, hardworking laborer. How many more like him lived in the Patch and other shantytowns throughout the city, barely surviving? Was Flannigan one of them?

ten

He hadn't been there when she sang her solo before the show. Why had she thought he would be?

The image in the mirror distorted, and Katie reached up and swiped her eyes. The tears seemed to come out of nowhere when she least expected them. She was getting altogether too much well-intended sympathy from the other members of the troupe, and she wasn't sure she could take any more of it just now.

The thing to do was pretend she didn't care a bit that Sam Nelson had turned out to be an intolerant, unfeeling cad. Only, she did care. Way too much. Worse than that, she wasn't sure he really was all those things. Maybe he was just ignorant and misled about the true conditions of the Patch. And she'd sent him away.

She jumped up before the tears could well up again. Her makeup would just have to do. Grabbing her maid costume from the rack, she lifted it high.

"Here, let me help you with that." Bridget took the costume and dropped it over Katie's head and shoulders. Katie felt a tug at her waist as her friend cinched the frilly white apron over the black dress.

Katie peered into the mirror and pinned the mobcap to her curls, the final touch to her maid ensemble.

She caught Bridget's frowning image in the mirror and turned.

"What's wrong? It's straight, isn't it?" Katie took a closer look in the mirror. The cap was perfect as far as she could tell.

"I'm sorry, Katie," Bridget choked out.

Katie's stomach tightened. "What? Is something wrong?"

"I wish I'd never told you about Mr. Nelson and Chauncey Flannigan. It's hurting you. And it's all my fault."

Katie began shaking her head even before her friend finished her sentence. "You've done nothing wrong. I needed to know."

"I'd give anything to take it back. I'd eat my words, I would."

"Bridget, you only told me the facts. And you were right to do so." Katie took her friend's hands and peered into her eyes. "Now stop worrying about it. I'm all right. Really, I am."

But was she? She left the dressing room and walked down the hall to the stage wing. At her cue, she took a deep breath and, smiling, walked on the stage. Would he be there? As though of their own accord, her eyes went once more to Sam's special seat. Empty. Disappointment washed over her. She swallowed deeply and focused on breathing normally. Of course he wasn't there. It was silly to think he might be. Determined to take control of her thoughts, she threw herself into the performance. If only she had more lines or more action during the performance. Anything to fill up the moments.

As soon as the show was over, Katie rushed through the wings and headed down the hallway.

"Hold on there a minute, Katie girl." She turned and forced a smile as her pa walked up to her. "You've been avoiding me all week, you have."

"Why, Father. Between here and the boardinghouse, we're together day and night." She threw him an innocent glance, hoping he'd buy it.

"Don't be blinkin' those eyes at me, Katherine Marie O'Shannon. You're knowing exactly what I mean. It's time we're having a bit of a talk."

Katie sighed. "All right, Pa."

"I thought we'd go for a walk after we get home tonight. How does that strike you?"

Katie nodded and headed for the dressing room. Going for a walk with her father didn't strike her that well, but she knew their little talk was inevitable, so she might as well get it over with.

At least it had cooled a little by the time Katie and her father set out from the boardinghouse.

"Ah, nothing like the night air to fill a man's lungs before bedtime."

Katie watched, startled as her father took a deep breath. "Pa, do you think that's—"

Her warning was interrupted by her father's fit of coughing. She pounded him on the back as he wheezed and coughed in an attempt to breathe.

Finally, the spasms lessened, and he sucked air in between gasps.

"Are you all right?"

He nodded and waved his arm in her direction.

She waited until he was breathing normally again.

"It could be this night air isn't quite so good for the lungs as it used to be." He laughed, and Katie joined in with relief.

"Let's sit on that bench for a few minutes, Father, till you get your breath back." She guided him toward the small wrought iron bench that sat beneath the lamp at the corner.

"A good idea." He stretched and sighed as he leaned back on the bench.

They sat in silence for a moment. Katie waited, knowing he'd speak as soon as he collected his thoughts. The space between her shoulder blades tightened as she anticipated his scolding.

"Now then, daughter. It breaks my heart to see you moonin' over that young fellow."

"That's not what I'm—"

"Yes, it's mooning you've been doing. No doubt about it."

His tender smile warmed her heart, even while she dreaded this discussion. "I suppose."

"It's probably all for the best, you know."

Katie frowned. "I thought you liked Sam."

" 'Tis true, I did. Everyone knew I liked him. But lately something's been weighing on my mind." He paused and squinted up at the lighted gas lamp.

"I don't understand."

"Katie, dear, all the weeks he was coming to call, did Sam ever ask you to his home? Did he ever mention wanting you to meet his family?"

Pain, as from a knife, sliced through her heart. She'd thought of it. The possibility that Sam was trifling with her. Having some fun with the showgirl. But every time the ugly thought had pierced her heart, she'd pushed it away. She'd told herself there was a reason he hadn't asked her to his home. The time simply wasn't right yet. But deep inside, she'd felt fear. And now, her father had put her fear into words.

Unable to bear the thoughts bombarding her, Katie jumped up and ran toward home.

⁂

As he drove through the streets of the Patch, Sam was struck again by the abject poverty. How could there be hope in such a dismal place? The encounter with O'Hooley had brought a drastic change in Sam's outlook. While still holding reservations about Flannigan's honesty, he nevertheless looked at Conley's Patch with new eyes.

A little girl stood near the filthy canal in front of the house next to Flannigan's. Two other children, one about her size and the other one bigger and a head taller, stood by her.

Sam pulled up in front of Flannigan's and watched as the two girls crowded the little redhead closer and closer to the edge. Sam jumped from his carriage and ran toward the children. But he was too late. He watched in horror as the little girl tottered on the edge of a board for a few seconds then fell with a splash into the sewer.

When the two children noticed Sam charging toward them, they took off down the street. Sam jumped into the filthy water and grabbed the sputtering child by the shoulders. Tossing her to safety, he pulled himself out, dripping with slime.

The little girl stared at him, unmoving. He looked around helplessly. Where was everyone? Didn't anyone see what happened? Stooping down beside her, he gave her a gentle smile. "Where do you live, sweetheart?"

Her eyes widened at the sound of his voice, and tears poured out over her grimy cheeks. She raised a small finger and pointed to the house next to Flannigan's. He gave her a puzzled look. She seemed to be glued to the spot. Would she scream if he picked her up?

"Is it all right if I carry you home?"

She stared silently for what seemed to Sam like forever then nodded her head and raised her little arms toward him. He lifted her and stood. As he walked toward the house, warmth ran from his arms straight into his heart. Who could have known it would feel like this to hold a child in his arms?

Before he could step up to the porch of the shanty, he felt a tug on his collar.

"Ma's over there." She pointed toward the house next door.

"Your mother is at the Flannigans'?"

She nodded, so Sam turned and walked across the hard earth and sprigs of weeds that passed as a yard. When he stepped onto the Flannigans' porch, he could hear voices through the closed door. At his loud knock, the voices stopped, and almost immediately, the door swung open.

Mrs. Flannigan stood and stared, glancing from Sam to the child, her eyes wide.

"Oh! What in the world? Margaret, you'd best come here." She stood back and motioned for Sam to enter.

"Betty!" The woman rushed forward to take the child from his arms. "What happened to her?"

"I'm afraid she fell into the sewer."

She examined the child from head to toe and then looked at Sam. When she spoke, her voice was a hushed whisper.

"You jumped into that nasty muck to save her. How can I ever thank ya?"

"I'm sure anyone would do the same. And I don't think she was in any real danger."

"Betty, where are the Morgan girls? Beth was supposed to be a watching you."

Sam watched in admiration as Betty ducked her head and closed her lips. She wasn't going to tattle. Sam, however, had no compunction at all. "If you mean the pigtailed tyrant who crowded her over the edge, she and another little girl ran off down the street when they saw me."

The woman's voice rose with anger. "You mean Beth pushed her?"

"Not exactly. But she might as well have. The little monster kept crowding her toward the edge until she fell in. I saw the whole thing."

The little girl's voice shook. "B-B-Beth said I had to walk the plank."

Sam's heart wrenched with sympathy, and he hoped the would-be pirate would get what she deserved.

"Mr. Nelson, thank you so much. I'm beholden to you. Now I need to get my child home and get her cleaned up."

How did she know his name? Then it hit him. "You're Mrs. Thornton, aren't you? Bridget's mother."

"That I am. Now I must be getting home."

"Sarah, dear, don't be leavin' Mr. Nelson to stand there in those filthy clothes." Sam looked in surprise at Chauncey Flannigan. He sounded almost friendly. "Get him some water to wash up, and he can borrow my Sunday suit."

"Thank you, Mr. Flannigan. I'm not going to argue with you about that. I'd hate to drive home in this mess. But your Sunday suit won't be necessary. Anything will be fine."

Fifteen minutes later, somewhat cleaner and wearing the Sunday suit in spite of his protests, Sam sat at the Flannigan table and shared a pot of tea and tried his first bowl of Irish stew.

"Mr. Nelson, we've been so caught up in little Betty's adventure that I haven't asked your reason for being in the neighborhood."

Sam hesitated. Why exactly was he here? He wasn't sure. He only knew that after his experience with O'Hooley, he had to hear Flannigan's account of the accident again. Because when he'd come before, he had already judged this man guilty. This time he came with an open mind. "Mr. Flannigan, you don't owe me a second chance, but I would like to hear your side of the story again. I can't say if I'll change my mind about this case or not, but I promise to listen this time without a preconceived idea of the truth."

"Ah well, I may have misjudged you, too. Anyone who would jump into the sewer to save a child can't be all bad."

eleven

"Runnin' late, are ye?" a toothless old man teased, setting off laughter among the folks around them, as Katie made her way past the crowd. The ragtag line of hungry-eyed people ran all the way around the corner and up the sidewalk to the door of the soup kitchen.

Katie grinned and continued to smile and joke with those she recognized as she worked her way forward. How some of these poverty-ridden people could find a laugh or a smile in the midst of their drab lives constantly amazed her.

She squeezed through the front door, hoping she hadn't thrown off everyone's schedule by being so late. Morning rehearsal had gone over by nearly a half hour, and she'd had to scurry to get here at all before the lunch rush was over. By the looks of the crowd, there was still plenty of time to help.

She pressed her way across the room and into the kitchen.

Mrs. Carter stood by the stove, spooning chili from the huge cauldron into a large serving pot. "Oh, thank goodness. Grab that container on the table, please, and take it out front."

Katie got the pot of soup out just as two more emptied. She slipped it into one of the empty places, ladled hot mixture into a bowl, and handed it to a young boy who stood licking his lips.

"Thankee, ma'am." The boy took the soup and moved to stand before Mrs. Gilrich, another volunteer, who handed him a hunk of bread.

A bent, white-haired woman stepped up to the counter. She accepted the dish with a shaking hand and started to walk away, passing up the bread as she balanced the bowl of soup in one hand and leaned on her cane with the other.

Katie's heart lurched. She hung the ladle onto the rim of

the pot and stepped around the end of the counter. Grabbing a piece of bread, she hurried to the elderly lady. "May I please help you, ma'am?"

The woman relinquished the bowl and followed Katie to an empty place at a table in the center of the room. Katie placed the food on the table and smiled. "Promise you'll call to me if you need anything."

A twinkle appeared in the faded blue eyes. "Thank ya, lass. You're verra kind."

Shaking inside, Katie rushed back to the food line. *Dear God, how many of these old people are homeless and starving?*

By the time things slowed down and Katie glanced over to check on the woman, she had already left. Sadness washed over Katie. Did the poor old woman have a home? Or was she sleeping in an alley somewhere?

When Katie arrived back at the theater for the afternoon performance, she felt a familiar squeeze in her chest. Sam hadn't been to the show since she sent him away, but a day didn't pass without her wondering if he'd show up. Strange that her thoughts hadn't turned to him even once while she was helping at the soup kitchen.

Perhaps if she threw herself into her charitable work and her performances, she wouldn't spend so much time grieving. And why should she be distressed over a man whose only interest in her had been that of a trivial flirtation? She'd been naive and foolish to think he really cared for her. A twinge of uncertainty wiggled its way to the forefront of her thoughts, right along with a vision of Sam's deep brown eyes. Eyes that had glanced at her with what she thought was love.

That night, Katie played the part of Rose the maid with an intensity that drew curious glances from her friends. She didn't look at Sam's empty seat a single time.

She left the stage and headed down the hall. If she changed quickly and left the theater before the others, she wouldn't get trapped into a conversation with anyone.

"Hold on a minute, Katie." Mr. Harrigan touched her arm as she rushed past him. "I noticed you really got into your role just now." His smile was kind, so perhaps she wouldn't have to deal with anything but a few words of friendly camaraderie.

"Thank you, sir."

"It's okay to put yourself into the part, but try to keep it as close to the way it's written as possible." His eyes twinkled as he patted her shoulder and walked off.

Katie put her hands to her burning cheeks. Oh dear. If Mr. Harrigan noticed, everyone else surely did, too. They'd surely know the reason for overplaying her role.

She walked into the ladies' dressing room and found it full. So much for getting out ahead of everyone.

Giving up on her idea to avoid company, she walked back to Ma Casey's surrounded by friends. Friends who, to her relief, didn't mention her performance.

A few minutes before time to return to Harrigan's for the evening show, Katie and several other members of the troupe were relaxing in the parlor when a knock sounded on the front door. A moment later, Rosie Riley stood in the doorway. "Katie, it's Mr. Nelson. He's asking for you."

Feverish heat shot from Katie's head all the way down to her toes. She cast about for the right words. "Tell Mr. Nelson I've no wish to see him." Katie almost choked on the words. Did she really mean it?

Rosie threw her a worried look. "Are you sure?"

"Yes, I'm sure." Her whispered answer rang like a knell of death in Katie's ears.

Rosie turned and left the room, and Katie rushed to the window. So what if everyone was watching? She didn't care.

She peered through the lacy curtain and watched as Sam turned and walked away. Her stomach tightened. The dejected look on his face reflected the ache in her heart.

❧

Sam nudged his horse, urging him toward the river. He'd spent most of the morning at Conley's Patch talking to Flannigan's friends and neighbors. Story after story of the man's kindness and helpfulness to others were repeated as Sam went from house to house. The main two qualities that emerged were that Chauncey Flannigan was as honest as the day was long and that he was a hardworking man who provided for his wife. Sam also learned that the Flannigans' only child, Patrick, had died on the boat coming over from Ireland four years ago.

The Chicago River wove its way through the city, cutting it in two. So far, most of the fires had broken out on the other side. This side of the river was a hodgepodge of warehouses, stores, and other businesses, with a line of small frame houses where children played. Farther down, in the other direction, lay the docks where riverboats loaded and unloaded both passengers and goods to be hauled downriver. But on this stretch, Howard's Warehouse and Lumberyard took up an entire block.

Sam hitched his horse in front of the lumberyard and made his way through stacks of wood and piles of sawdust. The sounds of dozens of saws rang throughout the huge open-air shed.

Two men, bending over a sawhorse, looked up as Sam approached then returned to their work. Sam cleared his throat, and they both looked up again. One middle-aged man with a beard that reached almost to his collarbone frowned. He spat and a wad of something landed by Sam's foot. "Can I do somethin' for you, mister?"

Sam took a step away from the disgusting glob and shot a look at the speaker. "Maybe. If you were a witness to Chauncey Flannigan's accident."

The man's companion sent a startled look in the direction of the main warehouse.

"Well, now," the bearded worker drawled, "it depends. Who wants to know?"

Sam wasn't sure how to answer, but he decided to be forthright. "I'm representing Mr. Howard, but my main concern is to find out the truth about what happened."

The other worker turned and walked over to another group of men, speaking to them in hushed tones.

The bearded man stared at Sam, working his jaw. He turned and spat. At least this time not in Sam's direction. "I don't reckon we saw anything." He turned his back and headed over to the huddle of men.

Sam stared after the old-timer. That didn't go very well. If the men knew anything, they weren't talking. If Sam was reading them right, they appeared more nervous than antagonistic.

Stacks of lumber, some reaching nearly to the ceiling, stood around the shed. He eyed them as he passed through on his way to the warehouse door. There didn't appear to be any sort of restraints on them, and although Sam had no prior experience as reference, the whole area seemed unsafe to him.

A wide gaping door with a gate hanging in the air above served as passage for smaller stacks of lumber being carted through from the lumber shed. Sam veered to the left and went though the smaller door and into the warehouse.

A man in a business suit looked up from a ledger he held in his hand. "Can I help you, sir? I'm Jonas Cooper, the manager."

Sam walked over and held out his hand, which the man took. "I'm Sam Nelson, the attorney representing Mr. Howard in the Flannigan case. I wonder if I could speak to the workers and get a clearer picture of the accident."

Lines appeared between the man's eyes as he frowned. "You say you're Howard's attorney?"

"That's right." Sam nodded.

The man stood. "Well then, I believe you have the testimony of the witnesses here and at the tavern where Flannigan got hurt in a brawl. That's all you need. Our men don't have time to talk. Anyway, no one saw anything except the ones you have on record." He rocked back on his heels and gave Sam a determined look. "I think you'd best go back to your fancy office and get to work on the case."

Sam gave the man a wry smile, thanked him for his time, and left through the door to the lumber shed. Mr. Howard's foreman bore a startling resemblance to his employer. In personality at least.

But Sam wasn't going to be put off that easily. Turning his steps toward the lumberyard, he squared his shoulders. He had a job to do, and he was determined to get to the bottom of this situation before he was forced to accept the sworn statements of men whom he increasingly suspected of lying for the establishment.

When he stepped into the lumber shed, he darted a look around, hoping one of the workers would change his mind and talk to him. But of one accord, they averted their gazes. Disappointed, Sam left, got into his carriage, and clicked to his horse.

He skirted the Patch, choosing instead to go in the direction of the docks and cross the Clark Street Bridge to get to his office. He'd had enough of Conley's Patch for today. He left his carriage at the livery and walked around to the Nelson building.

Charlie looked up and appeared relieved to see him. He handed Sam a stack of papers six inches thick. "Your father wants you to take care of these documents. They're in relation to a custody case he'd like for you to do some research on." Charlie grinned. "In your spare time, of course."

Sam took the papers and locked them in his file cabinet then headed for his father's office. The custody case could wait until later.

It was time he and his father had another talk. Something wasn't right at Howard's warehouse. And he had a hunch it involved Chauncey Flannigan's accident. Sam wouldn't make a decision without facts, but his intuition told him Howard and his witnesses were lying about the accident.

And after their talk, Sam intended to make another attempt to see Katie.

twelve

Katie almost gasped when she came out onstage for her solo and saw Sam, first row, center seat, as though he hadn't missed a single show. She felt her heart pounding, and from the way his eyes brightened, he'd noticed the effect his presence had on her, too. The grin he tried to hide sent her pulse racing. And her number tonight was a love ballad. How in the world was she going to get through it?

The first note was a little shaky, but Katie managed to relax her throat and sing without choking. However, no matter how hard she tried, she couldn't keep her eyes from drifting his way before she left the stage. Warmth washed over her at the expression in his brown eyes. So convincing. If he wasn't in love with her, he should have been on the stage himself.

She hurried to change into the maid costume. Every time a noise sounded by the door, she started. She hurried into her costume and headed back to the stage wings, dragging Bridget with her. "Look and see if he's still there." The panic in her voice matched what she felt.

Bridget tiptoed out onstage and peeked through a crack in the curtain then drew back and walked softly across to Katie, who had twisted her handkerchief so tightly it left marks on her hands. "He's there all right. And starin' right at the stage as though he can see straight through the curtains."

Katie leaned toward Bridget, and the girl grabbed her shoulders to steady her. "Here now, don't you go a-faintin'."

"I won't." Katie took a deep breath and steadied herself. She knew if she messed up during the performance, Mr. Harrigan wouldn't trust her with a bigger part later. Not that she cared very much at the moment. She simply wanted to get through the show and back to the dressing room. Would he come? And if he did, should she see him?

Katie played her part, saying her one line without a mistake. But by the time the play was over, her curls were plastered to her forehead.

After the show, she hurried back to the dressing room, got into her street clothes, and removed her makeup, listening all the while for a knock at the door.

Thirty minutes later, everyone had cleared out except for Katie and Bridget, who refused to look her in the eye.

Katie stood. "Well, that's that."

"We could wait a little longer, if you're wantin' to."

"No, if he was coming, he'd have been here long ago. Let's go home." Katie trudged down the hallway, beside Bridget, to the performers' entrance. She pushed open the door and stopped in her tracks.

A tall form leaned against the building. Even in the darkness she recognized him.

Stepping through the door, she waited for Bridget to follow her. Her friend's sharp intake of breath revealed that she'd seen him, too.

He removed his top hat and stepped in front of the girls. "Miss O'Shannon, Miss Thornton."

"Good evening, Mr. Nelson," Bridget stammered and curtsied.

Katie remained silent, her eyes lowered. She was pretty sure she couldn't have spoken if her life depended on it.

"Miss Thornton, I had the honor of meeting your mother and sister yesterday."

"Oh, did me mum seem well to ya?" The eagerness in Bridget's voice revealed her concern at being away from her family.

"They both seemed quite well. I met them at the Flannigans' when I was visiting there."

Katie jerked her head up. "You went to see Mr. Flannigan again?"

"Yes. If you'll permit me to see the two of you home, I'd like to talk to you about it." He smiled. "As well as other things."

Katie bit her lip then lifted her eyes and looked into his. "I'm not sure that would be wise."

"I promise to leave without protest whenever you ask." His sincere gaze set her heart to pounding again.

"Oh, Katie, what can it hurt?" Bridget piped up. "I for one would rather ride than walk. My feet are killing me."

Katie threw Bridget a sideways glance. Her friend wasn't fooling her a bit. Grateful to her for making it easier to accept Sam's offer, she nodded.

"Very well, Mr. Nelson. I don't suppose there's any harm in accepting a ride." She blushed as he offered one arm to her and the other to Bridget.

The ride to Ma Casey's was a little uncomfortable as Sam had put both girls in front and she was squeezed close to his side. The very idea. He did that on purpose. She pressed her lips together as she felt a smile coming on.

They pulled up in front of the boardinghouse, and as soon as Sam had helped Bridget down, she yawned and said she was going to bed. Before Katie's shoes hit the pavement, the front door had closed behind her friend.

Katie and Sam sat on the wicker chairs on the porch, and she listened, mesmerized, as he related the incident with O'Hooley and then his talk with Flannigan. She could see that although he said he hadn't totally decided on his course of action, his heart knew the truth.

"I've spoken to my father about conditions in the Patch. I think he believes I'm exaggerating, but at least he's agreed to ride over with me tomorrow and take a look for himself. I don't know how much good he could do, but he does have some influence in the city."

"What about Mr. Flannigan? Are you still going to represent his employer?" She held her breath as she waited.

"Father is adamant that he won't drop the case without

proof that Howard and his witnesses are lying."

"Well, can't you take Mr. Flannigan's case yourself?"

He shook his head. "I can't go against my father. But I promise I'll do everything in my power to uncover the truth."

It wasn't until Katie was lying in her soft feather bed that she realized the matter of his not inviting her to meet his family was still unresolved. She flopped over onto her side. Next time she saw him, she'd ask him right out. She had to know if Sam was ashamed of her for being on the stage. Or even for being half Irish.

❧

The carriage dipped and swayed over the dry, rutted streets of the Patch. Neither Sam nor his father had spoken since they'd entered the filthy shantytown. Stealing a glance at his father, Sam noticed his mouth was tight and the creases at the corners of his eyes were deeper than usual. Sure signs that he was disturbed.

They turned onto Flannigan's street. As they neared his house, Sam turned to his father. "The last time I was here, a little girl fell into that sewer." Sam paused then added for effect, "I jumped in after her."

"What?" The astonishment on his father's face spurred Sam on. "Yes, Flannigan gave me clean water to wash with and his Sunday suit to wear home. His wife gave me Irish stew."

"You ate with these people?" Sam thought he may have revealed too much. His father's face had reddened, and a vein protruded at his temple.

"Calm down, Father. Their home is spotless." As an afterthought, he added, "And the soup was very good."

"Do you realize you're not supposed to fraternize with the enemy?"

"The Flannigans are hardly the enemy, Father, and I was merely attempting to discover the truth. If you want the truth, I am sure Howard is lying. And so are his so-called witnesses."

"Sam, you do realize if you continue down this route, I'll

have to remove you from this case." He glared. "Promise me you'll stay away from Flannigan."

"Father, you're an honest man. I can't believe you don't want me to search for the truth."

"I've told you before. If you can bring me proof Howard's lying, I'll send him packing. But as long as he remains our client, we're honor bound to do what we can to win this case for him."

"Very well, Father. I'll find you that proof."

"I've seen enough. Turn around and let's get back to the office. This place is a disgrace, no doubt about that. But I don't see what I can do about it. And we've both got work to do."

Sam complied, and they drove back to the Nelson building in silence. He knew his father wouldn't take him off the case. But he didn't like being at odds with him over anything.

He pulled up in front of the office to drop his father off before driving the carriage to the livery. As he watched his father step onto the sidewalk, he noticed for the first time the older man moved more slowly than before. He'd never thought of his father getting old.

Eugene stepped out onto the sidewalk, put his hand on the side of the carriage to steady himself, and peered up at Sam. "Put Davis on it. I'll give you two weeks."

Elated, Sam leaned over and grabbed his hand. "Thanks, Father. If I don't find anything by then, I promise I'll drop the subject and represent Howard to the best of my ability."

Eddy Davis had done work for the Nelson firm before. When they needed investigative work done behind the scenes, so to speak. Sam drove to a livery down near the Clark Street Bridge, left his horse and carriage, and then set out on foot to a small dive down by the docks.

Even on this sunny afternoon, Sam had to stop just inside the door of Gert's Club until his eyes could adjust to the dark. The smoky cabaret was almost half full even this early. Sam crossed the small dance floor and rounded the corner by the counter. A door in back led to a line of offices. He tapped on the door of the last one and entered a tiny, cluttered room.

Eddy Davis sat with his feet propped up on a mammoth desk. "Hey, Sam. Haven't seen you in years." He swung his feet off the desk and stood, reaching his arm out.

Sam shook his hand and grinned. "It's only been two months, Eddy."

"Oh yeah. That divorce case. Some old bird's young wife cheatin' on him." He slammed his hand on the desk. "So, what can I do for you?"

Sam picked a piece of paper and a pencil from Eddy's desk and wrote Howard's name. He slipped the paper across to Eddy.

In spite of the shady accommodations and Eddy's less-than-respectable appearance, Sam knew he was professional and thorough on the job. And one of the best-kept secrets in Chicago. You had to know someone who knew someone to obtain Eddy's services.

The man glanced at the name and whistled. Placing both hands on his desk, he leaned over and raised both eyebrows. "This ain't no cheatin' wife case."

Sam shook his head. "I need everything you can find on him. Past and present. And I need it fast."

Eddy whistled again. "This is heavy stuff, Sammy boy."

"You'll be well paid."

"Yeah. If I'm around to spend it."

Sam laughed. "You're kidding, of course."

Silence fell on the room. Heavy. Ominous. Could there really be danger?

A laugh exploded from Eddy's mouth. "Sure I am. Just kiddin'. I'll get right on this for you."

Relieved, Sam shook his head and grinned. He gave a sizable retainer to the detective and left, with a promise from Eddy to report to the office every day.

Eddy almost had him going this time. The man had a sick

sense of humor. But a moment of doubt worked at Sam's mind. For just a moment, Eddy had sounded afraid. Impatient, he clamped down on his imagination. Eddy would be fine. He was the best detective in town.

thirteen

Katie pushed the needle into the satin fabric and pulled the thread through. She'd known this day would arrive sooner or later, but she'd hoped it would be a little bit later.

"Rosie, dear, it's grand to see you back. The show wasn't the same without you."

Rosie patted the puff across her face and laughed. "Don't be silly, Faye. I've been here every day, cheering you all on."

"Yes, but that's not the same, and ya know it."

Katie bit her lip to keep back the tears. She was happy that Rosie was fit and ready to take over her role as Sally. And this, of course, put Patsy back in the housemaid role. At least Katie wasn't complaining the way Patsy was. She wasn't about to make that kind of fool of herself.

Rosie stood. As she walked by Patsy, she smiled. "I thank you for filling in for me, Patsy. I've been watchin', and you did a wonderful job."

Katie lifted her eyes and glanced at Patsy. Surely the girl would be gracious.

"I don't know why I couldn't have continued with the part," Patsy snapped. "After all, as you admit, I did a good job."

A ball of anger clutched at Katie's stomach as she saw a pink flush wash over Rosie's face. Oh, how she'd love to grab a handful of Patsy's sleek black hair and yank it from her head. She looked at Rosie and was met with a smile and a shrug. Katie grinned.

"And you, Katie girl. . ." She placed a gentle hand on Katie's shoulder. "You're the talk of the town. Your singing is causing quite a stir."

"Really?"

"Yes indeed."

A flush of pleasure warmed Katie's face at the praise. "I love doing it."

"There'll be other acting roles for you, too. Don't you be worrying about that." With a smile and a pat on Katie's shoulder, Rosie took her leave. The room quickly emptied, leaving Bridget and Katie alone.

"You're not frettin', are you?" Bridget laid her sewing on her lap and peered at Katie.

"I'm fine." Katie smiled at her friend. "You don't need to be worrying over me about every little thing. Besides, this will give me more time for my work at the kitchen. And maybe I'll find other places to volunteer."

"Oh, Katie, I have some news for you. I forgot to tell you." The gladness in her eyes proclaimed her news was happy.

"What is it? Tell me."

"Benny O'Malley stopped by this morning with a note from me mum. They've formed a child care center of sorts. Mamie Todd is running it, with some of the young girls helping. She already has three little ones."

"Oh, that is good news! I wonder if there's anything we can do to help."

"No doubt about that. They'll be needin' blankets for pallets and kitchen stuff, too, I'm sure."

"Good, let's get right on that this afternoon. I'll ask Pa to help, too."

"You know somethin', Katie?"

"What?"

Bridget's lips puckered into a smile. "You have a lot more excitement in your eyes when you're talking about helping people than when you're talking about show business."

Surprised, Katie stared at her friend. Bubbles tickled her stomach as she wrapped her mind around her friend's words. It was true. She felt her eyes crinkle. "Bridget, I believe you're right. But that doesn't mean I'm giving up show business."

Bridget tossed her red curls and laughed. "I never expected ya would."

The girls went shopping as planned during the long afternoon break. Katie's father had been generous, so their arms were piled high with parcels when they climbed into a public carriage and headed to the Thornton home.

"Bridget!" The tiny version of Katie's friend ran pell-mell down the steps and flew into Bridget's arms, sending packages flying.

Laughing, Bridget swung her little sister around then set her down on the ground. "Now look what you've done, you little scamp. Start picking 'em up now."

A few minutes later, Katie and the two sisters dropped the parcels on Betty's little bed.

"Sister, I fell in the sewer, and a nice man jumped in and saved me." Betty was bubbling over with excitement.

"Ma, what's she talking about?"

Bridget's mother had come in from the other room, wiping her hands on a towel. She smiled at Katie and gave her elder daughter a hug. "I wasn't expectin' you until evening. You're still coming for the weekend, aren't you?"

"Of course, Ma. We brought some things over for the child care center. Now what's this about Betty fallin' in the sewer?"

Bridget's mother waved her hand and gave a loud, dramatic sigh. "It was quite a thing, let me tell you. Some other children crowded Betty over the edge of the ditch. Mr. Nelson jumped in and saved her. Carried her to the Flannigans' to find me." She shook her head. "He was a mess, he was."

Katie placed her hands on her cheeks, her eyes wide. "Do you mean to say Sam. . .I mean, Mr. Nelson. . .actually jumped into the sewer?"

"That he did. Plucked our Betty out of the slime and marched over to the Flannigans' with her in his arms." She smiled at her little girl. "He's a hero, he is."

Sam never said a word about it. Why hadn't he told her

about saving Bridget's little sister? Had he thought it would sound as though he were tooting his own horn?

Warmth and a tenderness she hadn't felt before filled her heart. He truly was a good man. Even if he should decide to continue representing Howard, she would still know that he was a good man.

Katie watched as Bridget tore open the packages and presented the goods to her mother, who watched with astonished eyes.

"Oh, you darling girls! I can't tell you what this means."

"Mrs. Thornton, if Mrs. Todd and the other ladies won't be offended, I think there are others who would be happy to sponsor this endeavor until you get things going."

"I don't think anyone would be offended. I know I wouldn't. This is to help our people. And I know you won't approach anyone who would try to bring shame on us."

Katie and Bridget got back to the theater just in time for Katie to run through her new song before the performance. When she walked out onto the stage, her eyes found Sam. He winked, and her heart fluttered. Then she began to sing.

a.

Sam slammed into his father's office and threw the folded newspaper on the massive oak desk. "They killed him."

"What? Who killed whom?" He picked up the paper and scanned it. "I don't see—"

"There. Right by that advertisement. It's Eddy."

"Davis?" He peered at the small print and read aloud: "'A body found beneath the Clark Street docks on Tuesday night proved to be that of Edward Davis, a private detective. The absence of money or other valuables lead authorities to assume Mr. Davis was the victim of robbery.'"

"It wasn't robbery, Father. You know it wasn't. He got too close to something illegal. It was Howard."

"You're making assumptions, Sam."

"Maybe. I don't think so. Eddy implied the case was

dangerous. Then he laughed and pretended to be joking. I should have known he was serious. Looking back, I can see it. But all I could think of was finding something on Howard." Sam tightened his lips and took a deep breath. "If it's murder, I'm going to find out."

"Don't do anything foolish. There's no proof Howard had anything to do with the death. It could have been a simple robbery as the police believe." He sighed. "And if it was murder, you could find yourself in danger. Leave it alone, Sam. Please."

Sam threw a short nod his father's way and left the office. He stopped briefly at his own desk to look over some files and then started toward the door.

"Sam, wait a minute." Jack was just leaving his office. "Where've you been keeping yourself? You're in and out of the office all day, and I haven't been able to catch you in weeks."

"Sorry. I've been really busy. How've you been?"

"Fine, fine." He lowered his voice. "I guess you're still seeing that girl."

"Shh. I haven't told my parents yet."

"What do you mean, yet? Why would you want to tell them and upset them? Unless. . ." He shot a worried look at Sam. "You're not serious about her, are you?"

"Jack, I'd love to stand and talk, but I have things to do. I'll see you later." Sam grinned to soften his words and left the building.

Driving toward the docks, he tried to set a plan of action. He had no idea how to start his investigation. "God, I could use some direction here."

The dock was teeming with activity as workers loaded and unloaded the boats that carried goods up the river and back. Sam tried to question a number of men who were willing to stop and listen to him. But if anyone knew anything about Eddy, he wasn't talking.

Discouraged, Sam walked to Howard's lumberyard and warehouse where he got the same response as before. He spotted the two men he'd spoken with in the shed the last time and walked over to them. "I don't suppose you men have thought of anything since the last time I was here."

The bearded one spat his glob of tobacco out of the side of his mouth. "Listen, fellow. If I was you, I'd get out of here and not come back. There's nothing for you here but trouble."

Realizing he wasn't getting anywhere, Sam turned to leave. He spotted two men by the warehouse gate, whispering. One pointed in his direction. Sam started toward them, but they turned away. Anger like a hot poker stabbed him as he left. They knew something. Some of them did, anyway.

He'd left his carriage in a livery across the bridge, so he headed there. The sound of footsteps caught his attention, and he turned to see a figure dart behind a building. Suspicious, he ambled on down the street, listening intently. This time, when he turned, he saw the man plainly. With long strides, he got to the man before he could duck behind another building. "Okay, why are you tailing me?" He grabbed the man's arm and frowned into his eyes.

"Hey, wait a minute. I'm not meanin' you no harm. I got a message for you." He jerked his arm away.

Sam gave a short laugh. "If you have a message for me, why were you sneaking around? Why not just give me the message?"

. "Cuz I don't know ya. That's why. Didn't want no fist in my face."

"Okay, okay. What's the message?"

The man looked around then leaned in closer to Sam. Lowering his voice, he said. "There's some of us what wants to help you. But we gotta be careful, ya see?"

Excitement shot through Sam like a bolt of lightning. "Yes, I understand."

"Okay then. Here's the deal. There's an old shed in back of

Wiley's Feed and Grain in the Patch. Be there at midnight. And make sure you're by yourself."

Before Sam could answer, the man turned and slipped around the corner. Should he follow him? Sam hurried to the corner and looked down the street, but there was no sign of the messenger.

Deep in thought, eager with a hint of dread running through him, Sam walked to the bridge and crossed over to the livery stable. Was he finally close to an answer to the Flannigan question? Would he discover something tonight about Howard's shady dealings, perhaps even something that would lead to the truth about Eddy's death?

Avoiding the office, he urged the horse toward home. He needed to calm down before facing his father's scrutiny. It wouldn't do for him to find out what Sam planned to do. He'd say it was foolhardy and probably forbid Sam to go. Right now, the one he needed to talk to was his mother. He couldn't tell her what he planned to do tonight, but he could ask her to pray with him.

Suddenly a vision of Katie's face filled his thoughts. Yes, it was time to tell Mother about Katie, too. She'd understand and perhaps help prepare the way for Sam to tell his father.

But not yet. First, Sam needed to get this other situation taken care of. Tonight, at midnight, he'd be waiting at a shed in Conley's Patch.

fourteen

"So you see, they need to get the child care center going so the women can work. They need more space. Even one extra room would help. The men can do the building. Once they get all the supplies they need, they can take care of it themselves."

"I think it's a wonderful idea." Rosie's eyes shone. "I get so tired of hearing about how lazy and worthless the immigrants in the Patch are. You can count me in. I'll do what I can."

Katie glanced at Bridget and smiled at the murmurs of agreement coming from the lips of the actresses and seamstresses. Rosie's enthusiasm had stirred up their interest.

By the time the curtain went up for the evening performance, most of the troupe from actors to stage crew had pledged to help with food and supplies to get the child care center on its feet.

With a light heart, Katie stepped out onto the stage. She glanced toward Sam's seat, expecting to see him smiling up at her. Empty. *Don't be silly. He's a busy man. Something must have come up.*

After the show, she said good-bye to Bridget, who was going home for the weekend. She watched the Harrigan's carriage pull away with Bridget inside. The weekends were long without her friend, even though Katie had her solos the next day.

She walked to the corner where her father waited for her. He held out his arm for her, and they walked down the plank street toward Ma Casey's.

The moonlight was bright tonight. There had been no fires this past week, and gradually the haze was lifting. Hope filled Katie's heart as it did the rest of the city. Perhaps the devastation was over for now. She asked her pa as much.

Scratching at his chin, he gave a shrug. "Well, it's still mighty dry. Just as dry as before. The little bit of sprinkling we had last Sunday isn't going to help much."

Katie sighed.

"But it's the third week in September. The rains are sure to come soon." He nodded. "Yes, no doubt about it. It always rains in September."

They walked in silence for a few minutes. Katie hoped her father was right. But the constant fires were frightening. How much longer before lives were lost?

Her father cleared his throat, a sure sign he had something to say that he knew she wouldn't like.

Katie's stomach tensed. Something about Sam, most likely.

"Daughter, I've got something I'm wanting to say." He continued to walk, looking straight ahead. "I know you like the lad. And I can't say I don't. It's a good thing you got over the arguing, but I still have the same concern as before." He took a deep breath and let it out loudly. "If he's serious about you, he'll be taking you home to meet his folks. If he doesn't do that soon, then he's just playing around with a pretty Irish lass."

Katie hated to consider the thought, but Pa was right.

"I know what you're saying, Da." A little choking breath emanated from her throat. "And you're right. I've already been thinking about it. And the matter will be settled soon, or I'll not be seeing him. I promise."

He patted her hand, and they stopped in front of Ma Casey's. Reaching over, he pushed back her curls and kissed her forehead. "That's the first time you've called me 'Da' since you were just a wee girl. It did my heart good."

"I love you, Da." She leaned into his big, comforting chest.

"And I love you, Katie girl. I'm praying your young man turns out to be true."

They walked up onto the porch and into the house.

❧

Sam clicked at his horse and sat up straight in the saddle. It wouldn't do to be too relaxed as he rode down the pitch black streets of the Patch.

He'd looked all along the main business district of the Patch but still hadn't found Wiley's Feed and Grain. It had to be on one of the side streets. He urged his horse around another corner and squinted his eyes to adjust to the difference in the blackness.

A curse sounded from down the street, followed by a scream and then a shout of bawdy laughter. As he drew near, his stomach churned. Apparently, the Patch's version of a prostitution district. Sam flipped the reins, the horse trotted to the next intersection, and they rounded the corner.

He pulled out his pocket watch and peered at the face but was unable to see the hands or the numbers. Spying a tavern at the end of the street, he spurred his horse into a gallop and pulled to a stop in front of the rundown shack. The hitching post was full, with three sorry-looking nags, so Sam tied his mount to a tree branch and went inside.

After the thick darkness of the outside, the tavern's dim interior was enough illumination to see fairly well. Sam made his way through a mass of whiskey-reeking men and, to Sam's dismay, a number of women as well. He stepped up to the scratched counter and started to pull his watch out then thought better of it.

"Name your poison." The man sported a patch over his left eye and squinted the other at Sam.

"I'd like to purchase a block of matches, please." Sam tossed a coin on the counter.

Without a word, the man turned and grabbed the block and laid it in front of Sam.

"Anything else?"

"I wonder if you could tell me where Wiley's Feed and Grain is."

The man pointed his thumb behind his head. "About three blocks back that way to Quincy then turn west. But they ain't open this time of night."

"Thank you." Sam elbowed his way through the crowd, having to steady more than one staggering patron before he got to the door.

Relieved to be out of the place, Sam loosened his horse's reins and mounted. He rode down another block and then stopped. Pulling one of the matches from the block, he used his thumbnail to strike it, holding his head back from the sulphurous fumes. The match head sputtered and flamed up with plenty of light to see his watch. Eleven thirty. Still enough time.

He rode down the street, turning at the corner, and headed in the direction the tavern keeper had indicated. His heart pounded in his chest as he rode the three blocks then turned onto Quincy.

Wiley's, which looked like a ramshackle barn, stood dark and forbidding, one of three buildings on the block. The other two appeared just as deserted.

Sam hesitated then urged his horse around the side of the feed store. About six feet behind the building, a small shed leaned to one side, its door hanging open.

Sam hesitated again. He could be walking into a trap. Something snapped, and he caught his breath. Careful, so his saddle wouldn't squeak, he looked around. Nothing was in sight. Maybe an animal.

He dismounted and stepped forward, leading his horse until he reached a clump of bushes where he tied the reins firmly. With nerves taut and senses heightened, Sam crept toward the shed. The rigid muscles in his throat ached, and he relaxed them, scoffing silently at his fear.

He kicked open the door and paused, ready to jump back at the slightest threat. His chest pounding, he stepped inside. The first blow glanced off his shoulder, but before he could turn, a fist hit his head sending pain through his skull. A blow to his stomach sent him to his knees. But they kept coming. His strength ebbed. His heart raced then slowed. Dizziness threatened to rob his consciousness. Then he fell forward, his face hitting the rough slab floor. Unable to move, he awaited the next blow and cried out when a foot to his side sent spasms through his ribs and back.

"Okay, that's enough!" A rough voice yelled, but not soon enough to stop one last blow from landing on his head.

"I said that's enough! We're not supposed to kill the guy. Remember?" Sam looked in the direction of the voice, but his eyes refused to open. He heard a grunt then the sound of something hitting the wall. Someone cursed. At least he wasn't the one who'd been thrown.

"Ouch. What'd you do that far? I wuz just havin' some fun."

"We ain't here to have fun. Come on."

Sam heard the door being flung open. Good. Maybe they were leaving.

He tried to push himself up, but his arm refused to move. He lay still as the voices of the two men grew fainter. . . .

He woke to an iron fist crushing his body. Pain shot through his head and behind his eyes from a constant jolting. He gasped. His eyes could only open a crack, but that was enough to see he lay in a wagon bed.

The wagon stopped. He lay still, afraid even to breathe. Hands grabbed him, one on his shoulder, the other by his belt, and heaved. Air gushed from between his burning lips as he hit the iron-hard ground. Then darkness came once more.

❧

"Mr. Nelson. Wake up."

Gentle fingers patted Sam's hands and then his face.

He groaned and tried to open his eyes. Through slits of light, he made out a man's shape.

"Sarah, hold the light closer."

Sam willed his eyes to open wider. Flannigan.

"Mr. Nelson, it's Chauncey Flannigan. We found you unconscious in front of the house. Do you know who did this to you?"

He groaned again, but words refused to pass through his dry, cracked lips.

"Never mind. We've sent word to your father. He should be here soon. Try to stay awake."

Sam drifted in and out of consciousness. Senseless words floated around him. Sometimes the straw mattress rustled beneath him. Other times someone gently lifted his head and poured cold water between his throbbing lips then laid his head down again.

"I need to let Katie know."

Sam started. He knew that voice. Even whispered. Bridget?

"You'll do nothing of the kind, young lady. There's not a thing she could do tonight. In the morning will be soon enough to be taking word to her." The voice, although quiet, was firm.

"Sam. Sam, wake up."

Sam opened his eyes.

His father towered over him. "I've brought Dr. Tyler."

Firm hands probed and prodded until Sam yearned for darkness to take him once more.

"A concussion's almost certain. Four broken ribs. Left ankle may be broken." The man paused. "If this gash had been a half inch to the left, he'd have lost his sight in that eye."

Relief washed through Sam. Dr. Tyler had treated him all his life. He was in good hands. With that thought, he closed his eyes, and the next thing he knew, someone had lifted him. Fear washed over him. "What?"

"It's all right, Sam. Mr. Flannigan is taking you to the coach. We're going home."

"But Katie. . ."

"Katie? Who is Katie?"

"Never mind."

The jostling ride home was agony as bolt after bolt of pain stabbed through Sam's body, and he yearned even for Flannigan's straw mattress.

Finally they stopped. Sam winced as Fred, the coachman, lifted him. Every inch of his body screamed as he was carried inside.

"Oh, Sam." The distressed voice of his mother cut through the pain. "Be careful, Fred. Eugene, are you sure he should be carried up the stairs? I could have a bed made up in the back sitting room."

"Amy, he'll be fine. Stop fidgeting, and let us get him to bed."

Sam's back touched his mattress, and he sank into the downy softness. He sighed. Nothing compared to a body's own bed.

"Come in, Nancy. Put the basin on the table. I'll take care of him." His mother's gentle fingers touched his forehead, smoothing back his hair. The swish of the maid's skirt filled the air before the door clicked shut.

Sam's eyes closed, and he surrendered to the comforting warmth of the wet cloth on his face.

"Was he able to tell you who did this?" his mother whispered. She must think him asleep.

"No." His father sounded grim. "But I have a pretty good idea who is behind it. And if I'm right. . ."

Sam struggled to push through the fog. He had to get out of bed and stop his father from going after Howard.

fifteen

Katie buried her head in her fluffy pillow to try to drown out the pounding. There, that was better. Oh no. There it was again. Arrgghh. What was that awful banging?

"Katie, wake up."

Bridget? What on earth?

"Katie!" Bridget's insistent voice was followed by more loud knocking.

Katie grabbed a wrapper and stumbled over to the door. She yanked it open, and Bridget tumbled in, almost losing her balance.

The girl gasped and fell onto the bed where she sat breathing hard. "Mr. Nelson's been hurt."

"What?" Katie blinked and tried to make sense of Bridget's words through her sleep-induced fog. "What did you say?"

Bridget took a deep breath and grabbed Katie's hand. "Mr. Nelson was attacked last night. Someone beat him up real bad and dumped him in front of Mr. Flannigan's house."

"Oh. . ." Fear shot through Katie. "He isn't. . ."

"Oh no. No." Bridget shook her head. "He's alive, and the doctor says he'll be all right."

"Where is he?" Katie grabbed her dress from the closet and threw her robe across the bed. "I must go to him."

"His father took him home." Awe crossed Bridget's face. "You should have seen it, Katie. Old Mr. Nelson drove into the Patch in this big black coach. Just like a fairy tale. Then he came marchin' in like a king, bringin' this fancy doctor with him."

"Oh." Despair crashed over her at this giant wall that rose before her. A wall that separated her from Sam. She dropped down onto the bed, the dress on her lap. "I can't go to his house."

"Why not?"

"Because I've not met his folks yet. That's why not." She bit her lip and blinked at the tears that welled in her eyes. "I don't know if they're even aware of my existence."

"Oh, Katie," Bridget murmured. "I'm so sorry. I forgot."

"Oh well." Katie forced a smile. "I'm sure he'll get word to me. . .somehow."

"Of course he will," Bridget said, patting Katie on the shoulder.

Rosie stuck her head in the door and gave Katie a scrutinizing look. "Are you all right?"

"Sure I am. I'm just fine." But the forced smile on her face wouldn't have fooled anyone.

"Ma sent me up to get you girls. Breakfast is on the table." She wheeled and headed for the stairs, the bottom of her skirt twirling around her ankles.

Katie stood. "Why don't you go on down and get your breakfast while it's hot? I'll be down as soon as I'm dressed."

"Oh, I have to get back to Ma's. I promised to go to church with her." She darted a glance at Katie. "Wouldn't you like to go with us?"

Katie sighed. Bridget knew she liked to rest on Sundays. "Not this time."

"All right." Her voice was soft with disappointment. "I'll be seeing you tonight then."

Katie watched her friend leave and sank back onto the bed. Nausea rose in her stomach at the thought of food.

The day dragged by as Katie dawdled around the parlor and out on the porch and waited for word about Sam. Perhaps Bridget would have news for her tonight. Although, she wasn't sure just how she thought Bridget would hear anything.

"Daughter."

As her father stepped out onto the porch, Katie looked up from the embroidery she'd been stabbing at aimlessly.

"You haven't eaten a bite all day." His forehead wrinkled with worry.

"I had some soup awhile ago, Pa. Remember?"

"Well now, I do recall you twirlin' a spoon around in your bowl. But I don't remember you putting anything in your mouth."

Katie swallowed past the knot in her throat. "I'm sorry."

He sat beside her on the wicker sofa and put his arm around her shoulders. "Now, now. And it's sorry I am to be fretting you. I know you're worried about young Sam."

Katie laid her head on her father's sturdy shoulder and let the tears flow. "If only I knew he was all right."

ঌ

The aroma of coffee and ham drifted to Sam's nostrils. He stirred and opened his eyes. He moaned and raised his hand to shield them from the bright light streaming into the room, stabbing at his eyes like a thousand knives.

"Sorry, son. Let me close the curtains." His father stood up from the wingbacked chair pulled up next to Sam's bed. Stepping to the window, he yanked the heavy curtains shut, blocking out the light.

"Thanks." The pain was milder now. Bearable. Sam took a deep breath. At least he could open his eyes a little more than a slit this morning.

"Well, you're a sight, son."

"I'll bet." He tried to grin, but his cracked lips protested. He ran his tongue over them and immediately regretted it as fire blazed across them.

"Could I have some water, please?"

His father held a glass to his lips, and he gulped the cool liquid.

"Here, your mother brought some salve for your lips."

He held out a flat jar, and Sam dipped a finger in the aromatic gel and rubbed it onto his sore lips. Ah. The soothing balm felt cool and soft.

His father replaced the lid and put the jar on the table.

Sam felt around his face, his hand touching several bandages. "Maybe I'd better see a mirror."

"Hmm. Let me save you the trouble." His father eyed him and shook his head. "Both eyes are black. You have a gash running from your mouth to the bottom of your chin and another from the left side of your forehead almost to your right eye. That was a close one. You also have numerous visible bruises, as well as many that aren't."

"Thanks. I appreciate your candor."

His father's hearty laugh landed like a sledgehammer against Sam's temples.

"Sorry, I forgot you have a headache. Probably will for a while."

"Probably. Father, you haven't tried to see Howard, have you?" Sam held his breath while he waited for his father's answer.

"I'm smarter than that, son." He sat on the edge of Sam's bed and nodded. "Much smarter. But it seems fairly obvious to me he was involved in this and maybe with Eddy's death. But knowing it and proving it are two different things. I have some people on it. In the meantime, I plan to have a talk with Howard. In my office."

"Be careful, Father. I don't know what sort of racket he has going, but if he'll kill for it and take a chance on having me ambushed when he surely should have known we'd suspect him, well, he's not playing games."

"And neither am I." The steel that Sam saw in his father's eyes confirmed the statement. "But I'm not sure he knows we're on to him or that Eddy was working for us. I think he just decided Eddy was getting too close. And the same about you. And now, that's enough unpleasantness for now." He slapped his hand on the bed. "What can I do for you while you're recovering? You must have unfinished business at the office I can help you with."

Sam looked thoughtfully at his father. Was this the right

time? Well, if not, it would have to be. Bridget was sure to have told Katie about the attack. She'd be worried sick. He had to let her know that he was alive and doing well.

"Actually, I'm caught up at the office. But I do need to speak to you about something."

"Anything. What do you need?"

Sam's head pounded, and his neck hurt. He forced himself to relax. How hard could this be? His father was a reasonable man.

"I've fallen in love with someone." He paused, weighing what his next words should be.

His father's mouth flew open, and he beamed. "Why, that's wonderful, son. Your mother will be ecstatic. She's wanted a daughter for years."

Sam smiled. "Yes, I know. I hope she'll be happy. I hope you both will."

"And why wouldn't we be? Who is this young woman you've been keeping from—" He stopped, and a wary look crossed his face. "Who is the young lady? Please don't tell me it's that actress at Harrigan's."

Sam stiffened. "If by 'that actress' you're referring to Miss Katherine O'Shannon, then yes, Father."

The bed rocked as Sam's father jumped up, his face red and twisted. "No. I won't see you ruin your life and career for a shanty Irish showgirl."

Sam clenched his teeth, ignoring the pain. He knew if he spoke now he'd say something he'd regret. He watched as his father paced the floor, ranting about showgirls in general and Irish ones in particular. He'd calm down in a minute.

Finally, the older man flung himself into the wingbacked chair and mopped his face with a handkerchief. "Sam," he said, his voice quieter than before, "surely you aren't thinking clearly."

Picking up the glass from the bedside table, Sam took a long drink. "Father, contrary to what you think, Katie isn't from shantytown, but even if she were, it wouldn't change anything. She's a wonderful girl. Kind, gentle, and a lady in both manner and action."

"Yes, yes, I'm sure she is. I'm sorry if I was hasty. I know you wouldn't fall in love with someone trashy. But there is also a question of social station. And whether we like it or not, that does matter."

"Not to me it doesn't. If our friends and acquaintances don't respect my choice for a wife, they aren't my friends."

"You say that now. But you may have cause to change your mind later."

"Won't you at least meet her?" A last ditch appeal, but maybe, just maybe, he'd agree.

"Not a good idea. It would only encourage her. That's not really fair to the girl."

He'd hoped his father would understand. But of course, it wouldn't be that easy.

"I won't give her up, Father. As much as it will hurt me to go against your wishes, I intend to marry Katie O'Shannon." He watched, with a tight chest, as his father stood and stalked from the room, letting the door slam.

Now what? He tried to sit up, but the pain in his ribs and head took his breath away. He had to find a way to send word to Katie.

Struggling, he stretched his arm toward the bell cord hanging by the bed. Agony pierced his entire body, but he finally grabbed it and pulled.

Within a minute, the door opened and Nancy stood there. She curtsied. "Yes, sir? What can I do for you?"

"Nancy, would you write a letter for me and have it delivered?"

"Of course, sir."

"You'll find writing material in the top drawer of my desk." He gasped as pain stabbed his ankle. How many more injuries did he have?

Nancy wrote as he dictated, and then with a promise to send the letter by one of the house servants right away, she left.

He leaned back on the bed and tried to sleep, but thoughts of Katie ran through his mind. Her soft curls, her wide blue eyes, the dimple on her cheek that dipped when she smiled. He didn't want to be estranged from the parents he loved. He had to somehow make them understand.

An hour passed. She should have his letter by now. He pictured her opening it. Saw the relief on her sweet face as she read that he was safe.

Sam sank back against the pillows and surrendered to sleep.

≈

The clock in the parlor seemed to tick louder and louder.

Katie listened, her dry eyes wide, staring at nothing. The others, including Bridget, had gone to bed an hour ago. She should, too. It was foolish of her to stay awake so late. After all, she had to go to the theater tomorrow morning. And anyway, of course he wouldn't send word this late. It was after midnight.

sixteen

Sam tossed the newspaper on the floor and leaned his head back against the high back of the chair. A slight breeze drifted through the open window, cooling his damp face. He closed his eyes and drifted.

A crow cawed loudly, bringing him back from a near doze. He twisted, trying to find a comfortable position. His pain had diminished, although his ribs were still sore and he could only hobble on his ankle. But the inactivity was driving him crazy.

He turned, leaned forward, and peered out the window. He'd lost count of how many times he'd looked, hopeful, out that window in the week since he'd sent the message to Katie. Why hadn't she come or at least inquired about him? Had he only imagined she returned his affection? No, he was sure she felt the same way he did.

Frustrated, Sam picked up the small bell on the side table and gave it a furious shake.

A moment later, Nancy tapped and opened the door. "You rang, Mr. Nelson?"

"Yes, come here, please."

The girl stepped lightly across the floor and stood in front of Sam. "What do you need, sir?"

"I know I've asked you before, but are you absolutely certain you sent the message I gave you last week?"

Consternation filled the girl's eyes. "Yes, sir, I'm sure. Just like I said before."

Sam sighed. He shouldn't be badgering the poor maid, but he couldn't believe Katie could be so unconcerned. "All right. Let's run through this step-by-step. You left the room with the letter."

She nodded, her curls bobbing below her mop cap.

"You called the messenger boy?"

Another emphatic nod."

"You placed it in his hands and watched him carry it away."

A flicker of something crossed her face, and she hesitated before answering. "Well, sir, not exactly."

At her worried look, Sam groaned. Something had gone wrong.

"Tell me exactly what happened, please."

"I took the letter downstairs and sent for a messenger boy, just like you said. Then, you see, Cook called me to take a fresh pitcher of lemonade to Mrs. Nelson and her friends, so I gave the letter to Franklin and asked him to give it to the messenger."

Sam frowned. Okay, this detailed account was a little bit different. Still. . . "Thank you, Nancy. Will you tell Franklin I'd like to see him at his convenience?"

"Yes, sir. Right away." She curtsied and walked away, turning at the door. "Did I do something wrong, sir?"

"No, no. Not a thing."

Sam leaned back in his chair. Franklin had been the Nelsons' butler since Sam was ten. He was extremely loyal to the family and very efficient. He'd have made sure the message was delivered.

The door opened. Sam turned, expecting to see Franklin, but his father walked toward him instead.

"Well, well. And how are you feeling this afternoon, son?" His father, always uncomfortable around convalescents, said the exact same words every time he entered Sam's room.

"Much better, thank you. Any news for me?"

The older man lowered himself into a chair across from Sam and shook his head. "Nothing yet. These things take time."

"Did you meet with Flannigan?" After meeting Chauncey and his family the night of Sam's attack, his father had decided he might have been wrong about the Irishman.

"No, I thought you might like to be in on that. After all, he is your friend."

Funny he'd say that. In spite of the fact that he'd only spoken with Flannigan a few times, Sam had found himself thinking of the man as a friend. He nodded. "Perhaps you could send someone to inquire when it would be convenient for us to go there."

"Yes, I'll do that."

"Father, I'd like to talk to you about Katie."

A guarded look shaded his father's eyes. "Not now, please, son. I've things that require my attention this afternoon. Perhaps later."

Disappointment surged in Sam's chest. He'd hoped to change his father's mind about meeting Katie. Sam suspected he was deliberately avoiding the subject.

"Wait," Sam called as his father walked to the door. "Will you see if you can find a crutch for me? I have to get out of this room and at least walk around the house."

"Yes, I'll get one from Dr. Tyler. But if you'd like, I can help you downstairs now. Perhaps you'd like to sit on the porch for a while. Get some fresh air."

"At this moment, there's not much I'd like better."

Leaning on his father's arm, Sam hobbled down the stairs.

"Eugene. What are you doing? Be careful with him." Sam's mother stood at the bottom of the stairs, her hands on her cheeks and distress in her voice. "Where are you taking him?"

"I'm fine, Mother." Sam struggled to speak after the difficult walk downstairs. "I simply need to get out of my room for a while. I'm going to sit on the veranda."

"Well, I don't suppose that will do any harm." She followed them out on the porch.

Sam sighed with relief as his father helped him settle onto one of the cushioned chairs on the wraparound porch.

The slight breeze that had drifted through his window earlier had disappeared. But though the air was still, the foliage of tall oaks and sugar maples, assisted by a curlicue overhang, shaded the porch.

"There. You should be comfortable enough here." Sam's father took his gold watch out and looked at the time. "I need to get back to the office. I'll send word to Flannigan, as you suggested." He kissed his wife and, with obvious relief, walked to the curb where Fred and his carriage waited.

"Would you like for me to read to you?"

Sam smiled at his mother as she patted him on the shoulder. "Thank you, Mother, but I believe I'll just sit here and watch the people go by." Although no one seemed to be braving the hot sun this afternoon. "However, if you'd send Nancy with a cold glass of lemonade, I'd be in your debt forever."

As Sam sat on the veranda drinking his lemonade, thoughts of Katie bombarded him. Had something happened to her? Or had her father forbidden her to contact him?

Franklin stepped out the door. "You wanted to see me, sir?"

"Yes, thanks. I wonder if you can straighten a matter out for me."

"I'll try, sir." Franklin's face was stiff. Sam could count on his fingers the times he'd seen the stately butler smile.

"Do you recall Nancy giving you a letter last week to pass on to a messenger boy?"

Something flickered for an instant in the butler's eyes, a muscle next to his mouth jumped, then his face straightened as though he'd suddenly donned a mask. "I'm sorry, sir. I can't recall. We have so many messages going to and fro."

Surprised, Sam stared. He had never known an incident involving the family in any way to have slipped the ever efficient butler's memory. He nodded, and Franklin turned and went back into the house.

Sam, puzzled, sat and stared across the lawn. What was this all about? Why would Franklin lie? Sam hated his suspicion of the elderly servant. Could it be that he truly had forgotten the incident? After all, he wasn't getting any younger.

❧

Why hadn't he contacted her? Katie peered out into the darkened theater. She'd hoped against hope he'd be in his seat as good as new with that quirky smile and a sparkle in his eyes. It had been nearly a week since Bridget had stumbled into her room with the terrible news of the assault.

Katie took a deep breath and sang her ballad for the second time that day. After her encore bow, she changed into her street clothes and slipped out the door. If she hurried, she could be back before the show was over. Father would never know she'd gone out on her own this time of night.

She stood outside the theater, considering the best way to get to Sam's house. If she used Harrigan's carriage, Father would find out. The trolley didn't go that far, and there might not be a cab available at the end of the line.

She bit her lip and eyed the carriage for hire standing nearby. She hated to spend the money, but with resolution, she hurried down the sidewalk, her heels tapping against the planks. Nodding to the driver, she gave him the address and got inside.

The carriage lurched, and Katie grabbed the side of the seat. Leaving the theater district, they passed the business district, bounced past cafés and boardinghouses then small, modest, private homes. They started up a slight incline, and the lighted windows of the larger homes revealed a more affluent lifestyle. Finally, they turned down a tree-lined street, with stone roads and sidewalks. How in the world did the residents keep their grass so green?

At the end of the street, a huge three-story brick house stood in royal splendor. The carriage turned into a circular drive and stopped in front of a wraparound porch. Light streamed out from nearly all of the windows, welcoming, inviting.

"Here ye be, miss. Do ye want me to wait for ye?"

Katie sat, unable to speak. Sam lived here? In this mansion? Her throat seemed to close up, and she swallowed with difficulty. What was she thinking? How could she believe a prince who lived in a house like this could be serious about her?

"Miss, I say we're here. And do ye want me to wait for ye?"

Perspiration popped out along the entire surface of Katie's face. She took a deep breath and stiffened her back. She'd come this far. She might as well complete her mission.

She stepped from the carriage. "Yes, please wait. I won't be long." *Unless of course, Sam opens the door and brings me in to meet his parents.*

She walked up the broad steps and across the porch to the heavy oak door. Lifting the knocker, she tapped it once and then once more against the smooth, rich wood.

The door swung open. A tall, well-dressed elderly man stood stiff and regal against the light of the hallway.

"Yes, miss, may I help you?"

Katie lifted her chin. "Is Mr. Sam Nelson at home? I heard he was injured."

The man looked at her in some surprise. Then an amused look crossed his face. "Young Mr. Nelson has been ill. He's much better now but is not receiving callers. However, if you'd like, you may leave a message."

Katie licked her lips. Her fingers tingled, and her legs felt as though they'd fold up any minute. "Yes, please tell him Miss O'Shannon inquired about his health."

She heard the door shut before she got to the carriage.

❧

"Katie, you've got to stop your mopin' around like this." Rosie, hands on hips, stood in the open doorway of Katie's bedroom.

"I can't help it. Why doesn't he contact me? Doesn't he know I'm worried?" A sob caught in Katie's throat. "Or maybe he's deathly sick and can't send word."

Rosie walked in and stood by the chair where Katie sat with tears streaming from her eyes. "Now, stop it. All this frettin' isn't helpin' a bit. And your father is beside himself with worrying about you."

"You don't understand. I can't help it, Rosie. What can I do?"

Rosie stood, a tender look on her face. She reached over and smoothed a curl back from Katie's eyes. "Sweet girl, have ya thought of talking to the Lord about it?"

Surprised, Katie stared at the older woman. Rosie went to church every chance she got. But Katie had never heard her talking about God before.

"You mean pray?"

"That's it. God loves you, whether you know it or not. And He cares about that young man of yours as well. Talk to Him, Katie girl." With another tender glance, she left the room, her steps light on the wooden floor.

Talk to Him? Was it really that simple? Just as Grandma used to say?

Katie slipped off the bed and knelt. "God? Are You there?"

seventeen

Katie's heels clacked on the boardwalk as she rushed down the street to the soup kitchen. The line seemed longer than usual, if that was possible. Gasping, she attempted to get a clear lungful of air. She wheezed and then coughed as she breathed in the acrid air. The short reprieve had ended, and fire after fire had thickened the air once more.

"Miss O'Shannon, thank the good Lord you're here. We have our hands full today. More families have lost everything."

Grabbing an apron and tying it over her dress, Katie took her place between Mrs. Carter and Sally Sloan, another volunteer, and started ladling soup into bowls. "Do we have enough to go around?"

"Yes, thankfully, I got word in time to cook extra." The director handed a chunk of bread to a little boy who walked away balancing a bowl in one hand and the bread in another.

Katie's heart lurched. The children broke her heart. She needed to do more to help them. But what? Her hours were already full, and she was pouring nearly every extra cent into the child care house at the Patch.

At least her busy schedule kept her from thinking about Sam. A deep peace about him descended on her after she'd knelt before God last Sunday, enveloping her like a warm blanket. She'd never felt like this before. As though God Himself walked with her all through the day. And although she didn't totally understand, she gratefully accepted His presence in her life.

"Eighteen of 'em so far this week." The old man's voice carried up the line, and Katie started.

"Yeah, I heard that, too. The fire department can't hardly

127

keep up with 'em." His statement was interrupted by coughing, and it was a moment before he continued. "The whole city's liable to burn down if we don't get some rain soon."

A little girl, her brown eyes filled with fear, glanced up at Katie as she waited for her food. "Are we gonna burn up?"

Katie winced at the panic in the child's voice. Why couldn't people keep their mouths shut around the little ones? She summoned her most reassuring smile. "Of course not, sweetheart. They're just being silly because they have nothing better to talk about."

The little girl giggled and followed her mother and another child to an empty place at one of the long tables.

God, please let what I just said be true. Send us rain. Please send us rain. She'd read this morning about the prophet, Elijah, praying for rain six or seven times before he saw a cloud in the sky. A shiver ran through her body. Had anyone in Chicago been praying for rain?

By the time the long line had been served and Katie had helped with cleanup, she had to rush to get back in time for her afternoon solo. Almost faint from the heat and the pain that now clutched at her side, she stumbled the last few steps to Harrigan's. Maybe she should drop out of the show. After all, there was so much work to be done at the kitchen, and there were other organizations that could use her help.

She walked through the back door of the theater, and her heart clenched. Another good reason to quit. As long as she was busy, she hardly had more than a passing thought of Sam. But the moment she walked through the theater door, a vision of his beloved face arose before her. The peace that she'd relied on for days suddenly lifted, and pain shot through her heart.

Oh, Sam, where are you?

❧

The familiar odor of sewer and cabbage assaulted Sam when he and his father stepped from the carriage in front of Flannigan's. He didn't like the idea of his father being at the Patch after dark, but it couldn't be helped if the workingmen were to be present. Slowly, he walked to the house where Flannigan stood in the open doorway.

"You're lookin' much better than the last time I saw ya. Glad to see ya on your feet. Come in. Come in." The Irishman shook their hands then stood aside.

At least two dozen men stood in the crowded room.

"Make way, so these gentlemen can sit down. Sarah, bring cold water. I'm thinking Mr. Nelson's needing it."

With effort, Sam smiled. Just the short walk to and from the carriage had sapped his strength. "I'll admit I've felt better, but I'm getting stronger every day."

The crowd parted so that Sam and his father could get to the chairs against the wall. Gratefully, Sam sank down onto the cane-bottom chair.

Flannigan handed glasses of water to Sam and his father. "I know ya got hurt because ya were seekin' the truth about my injuries. And I thank ya for that."

"Is anyone else coming?" Sam's father asked.

"No, sir. I think all are here who want to be."

The men dragged chairs in from the backyard. Apparently, they'd brought their own and stashed them outside while they were waiting.

When everyone was seated, Sam's father stood. "My name is Eugene Nelson. Some of you know my son, Sam. I believe most of you are aware of the fact that our firm has been retained to represent Jeremiah Howard in the matter concerning compensation for Mr. Flannigan's injuries."

He paused as a murmur passed through the crowd then continued. "Several incidents have recently occurred that cause me to question Howard's words as well as his business practices. Especially concerning safety in his warehouse and lumberyard. I understand a number of you work for him at one place or another."

Again murmurs. Relief washed over Sam that this time

they were murmurs of agreement, and the expressions on the men's faces, while not especially friendly, were at least not hostile.

His father continued. "I've asked Flannigan to relate what happened to him. When he's finished, if anyone has anything to contribute, I'd be more than happy to listen."

The room quieted as Flannigan stood and looked around the room. He told about the day of his injury and how he'd come straight home and fallen into bed, the pain in his head so intense he couldn't feel his other injuries. He told about his trip to the hospital and his treatment there, sharing the details of his injuries. Then he sat down.

One by one, others stood and told of their experiences as Howard's employees. Some had been injured on the job, although none as severely as Flannigan, but not one had received any sort of compensation. Several spoke of being cheated out of wages.

Sam's father nodded at him, and he stood. "If I can get enough evidence against Howard, my father has agreed to drop him as a client. In such a case, legally I won't be able to represent Mr. Flannigan. However, I will do what I can to bring the truth to light. I know an attorney who will take the case. It may not be possible to gain evidence for your past mistreatment, but testimony from witnesses such as yourselves could make a difference in the question of justice for your neighbor, although I've warned him there is no guarantee. But if enough of these incidents are presented before the court, it will almost force Howard to change his unjust and illegal practices in the future."

"So you want us to go to court and tell about our own experiences?"

Sam looked at the man in the back of the room who'd spoken. "If you will, it could help. We also need those of you who are willing to stand up for Mr. Flannigan's character."

"What if we lose our jobs? We've got families to support," a big man with a red beard and tight red curls called out.

Sam looked at his father. How could he answer a cry like this? What was it like to be trapped in a low-paying job with no way out? What did it feel like to know your small paycheck was all that stood between your children and hunger?

He listened as his father told the men he didn't expect anyone to do what he felt he couldn't do. Each would have to follow his own conscience. And no one would think less of those who refused to testify.

Sam and his father left and headed home. Home where Sam had enjoyed wealth and safety all his life. Where wonderful aromas of good food drifted from the kitchen and the smell of spices and perfumes wafted through the house. Where light shone into every corner and beauty filled every room.

"How do we help them, Father?"

"One case at a time. One step at a time. That's all we can do."

"That's what Katie said."

His father gave him a startled look, and some other expression crossed his face. But Sam was too tired to question him about it.

Sam leaned back into the soft, velvety cushions of the carriage seat. Now he understood why Katie worked tirelessly, trying to help the poor. Once she'd said, "We can't help them all, Sam. But we can help the ones before our eyes. The ones we know about. Little by little, we can make life better for some."

He had to see her. He was stronger now. Tomorrow he'd go to Ma Casey's. He'd find out why she hadn't answered his letter. He'd know, once and for all, if she still cared for him.

❧

Katie walked out of the theater with Bridget, and they trailed after the others so they could talk on the way to Ma Casey's.

"Tell me again why Sam and his father were coming to the Patch tonight?"

Bridget had gone home during the afternoon break to take

some things to her mother for the child care house. She'd bounced into the theater bubbling over with her news about Sam. "Like I told you before, Mr. Nelson and his father were supposed to go to Flannigan's tonight to talk to some of the men about Howard. I think they must have seen the light. I can't wait to talk to my mother and find out all about it."

"That's wonderful, Bridget." And it was. She'd longed for Sam to see the people of the Patch as they really were. But her heart ached, just the same. Sam was up and around, and he hadn't been to see her. The only explanation had to be that he didn't care for her anymore. If he ever truly had.

As they walked on, she listened to Bridget's excited and hopeful chatter about how the Nelsons could help the employment condition. Irritated, Katie bit her lip. To listen to Bridget, one would think Sam and his father were miracle workers.

Bitterness bit at her, and anger rose in her heart. All this time, she'd been picturing Sam at death's door, lying in bed, calling her name, only to discover he'd been at a meeting. How dare he trifle with her?

As soon as they arrived at Ma Casey's, she pleaded a headache and went to her room, her body stiff and tight. Flinging herself across her bed, she burst into tears. When the barrage ended, she sat up and rubbed her hand across her eyes. Shame flooded over her. *I'm just selfish. I never knew I was selfish. Oh, but Sam, I thought you loved me.*

She had to stop thinking of him. It was over.

A beam of moonlight caught her attention, and her eyes rested on the small white Bible on the table by her bed. She'd dug it out from her trunk the day after she'd turned her heart over to God. She'd carried it to church during the four years at Grandma and Grandpa's. But she couldn't remember ever opening it outside the church walls until last Monday.

Katie lit the lamp by her bed and picked up the Bible. Opening it to Psalm 1, her eyes scanned the words. She turned the page and devoured psalm after psalm. At the end, she started through Proverbs and read until her eyes were heavy and would no longer focus on the small letters. Yawning, she returned the book to the table and changed into her nightgown. As she sank into the feather bed, the words she'd just read flowed through her.

"Trust in the Lord with all thine heart; and lean not unto thine own understanding. In all thy ways acknowledge him, and he shall direct thy paths."

All right, heavenly Father, I'll trust You to lead me in the way You want me to go.

Her eyes closed, and she drifted off into sweet, peaceful sleep.

eighteen

"Where are you, Katie? Not here, I think. You've sung the wrong lines again." Donald Jones whirled around on the piano stool and frowned. "It's Saturday. You've got to hurry and learn this piece."

"I'm sorry, Donald. I guess my mind is wandering." Katie leaned forward, peering over her accompanist's shoulder at the sheet of music, and found her place. She wouldn't be singing the new song until Monday, so why was he in such a dither? She should probably be going through today's solo anyway.

Donald tapped his fingers against the piano and frowned. "You know I'll be away tomorrow for my little sister's wedding."

She'd forgotten about that. "Well, Rosie can play for me if I need to practice." Rosie often played for the troupe at night as they sat around singing old ballads.

"Oh, can she? Little girl, Rosie can't read a note. She plays the old songs by ear, which isn't going to help you." He turned back around and placed his fingers on the keys. "Let's try it one more time."

This time, Katie ran through the entire song without a mistake, and Donald turned and grinned. "I knew you could do it. Now, one more time."

They started from the beginning, and once more, Katie remembered her words and sang with no problems.

"Katie, I've called you twice." Bridget's voice rang out above the music.

Donald hit the piano keys, turned, and glared at Bridget. "Can't you see we're busy here, girl?"

Hands on hips, Bridget glared back. "Katie has a visitor, for your information."

"What? Who?" Katie's stomach lurched, and she started toward the hall.

"It's Mr. Nelson, that's who. I left him standin' on the porch. Shall I ask him in?" She cast a worried glance at Katie. "To tell you the truth, he's not looking so good."

Not looking so good? "Mercy, Bridget." Brushing past her friend, Katie rushed to the front door, her pulse racing. "Please come in. I can't imagine why Bridget left you standing out in the heat." Her voice sounded breathless even to her. Maybe he hadn't noticed.

Sam removed his hat and stepped inside, leaning heavily on a cane. Bridget was right. He was pale, and little beads of perspiration stood out on his face.

"Please come into the parlor. There's a little bit of a breeze coming through the window there." She ushered him in, sending Donald a pointed look.

"Don't forget, we need to run through the song again later." Donald left, and with a bit of triumph, Bridget followed, pulling the parlor door shut behind her.

Katie hoped Ma Casey didn't notice she and Sam were alone in a room with the door closed. She stood, tongue-tied, not knowing what to say, then realized Sam was still standing.

"Oh, please sit down. I'm so glad to see you are well enough to be up and around." *And finally here.* She pushed the thought aside. She shouldn't judge him until she heard what he had to say.

He sat on the end of the sofa, and she sat on a wingbacked chair facing him, her fingers twisting her handkerchief. He leaned back and took a deep breath, relief crossing his face.

Katie bit her lip. He must still be in pain. And she'd been blaming him for not coming. But why hadn't he at least sent word?

"I wasn't sure you'd want to see me," he said. Uncertainty crossed his face as he looked at her.

"Not want to see you? Why would you think that? Just

because you didn't acknowledge my visit or send word that you were all right?" She knew her voice sounded on edge, and although she truly didn't want to yell at him when he appeared so frail, he was the one who brought the whole thing up, wasn't he?

A puzzled look crossed his face. "What visit? And for that matter, I sent a letter that you chose to ignore. I assumed you had lost interest or were angry with me for some reason."

Katie gasped. What letter? "Chose to ignore? Why, I did no such thing. I never received one single, solitary letter from you. Not one."

"But. . .I dictated a letter to one of the housemaids, and she. . ." Confusion, followed by a flash of anger washed over his face. "And you mean all this time, you thought I hadn't tried to contact you?"

"What else was I to think?"

"Katie, I'm so sorry. I promise I did write and was assured my letter was sent."

Katie ducked her head to hide the tears that filled her eyes. He had written. She had no idea why she didn't receive the letter, but that was unimportant now. He did care about her. That was all that mattered.

Joy flooded her heart and radiated from the smile that wouldn't be held back. And needn't be. Sam's face told her all she needed to know.

She held out her hands, and he clasped them in his, holding on tight. "Katie." His voice broke over the one word. "I thought I'd lost you. And didn't know why."

Just then, the door opened, and Ma stood there with a wooden spoon in her hand, twisting her lips in an unsuccessful attempt to hide her grin. "All right, you two. I understand you've been apart for a while, but the door stays open." She frowned, albeit unconvincingly.

"Sorry, Ma. It won't happen again." Katie smiled as Ma left the door open. It seemed as though a smile was permanently fixed to her lips.

"Should you be up and about? Perhaps you need to go home and go back to bed."

"I'm fine. And wild horses couldn't drag me away from you now. I'll need to take things slowly for a while, and Father won't hear of my going to the office yet, but I'm getting plenty of rest. I promise."

Her heart soared. "All right. In that case, please tell me all about what happened and how you're doing." She listened in fascinated horror as he told her of the ambush but clapped her hands together when he spoke with admiration and respect of Chauncey Flannigan.

"I do have one request to make of you, Katie. Please don't be angry. But I feel it's unsafe for you to continue your work in the Patch."

She took a quick breath, and he held up his hand. "I know how important the work is to you, and I respect that. But isn't there some way you could help in the background without actually going into the neighborhood?"

"I don't see how. Or why I should. The people there need all the help they can get, and no one has harmed me."

Sam closed his eyes for a moment. When he opened them, she saw the worry they held.

"Crime is high in the Patch. There are very few police officers even in the daylight hours and none at all at night. It isn't safe for you there." He gave her a pleading look. "Please, Katie, I couldn't bear it if anything happened to you."

Silent for a moment, Katie considered his words. Of course she'd never give up her work. But perhaps she did need to be more careful. "I'll agree to this much. I won't go there after dark. And I'll take someone with me in the daytime."

He breathed deeply then nodded. "All right. That relieves my mind some. But please remain cautious at all times."

"I will, Sam. I promise." She looked deeply into his eyes and smiled.

❧

Sam drove home, his eyes shooting flames. He stormed into the house, his cane thumping loudly on the hardwood floor of the foyer.

"Franklin! Nancy!" he shouted. "Come here!"

"Sam, what's wrong?" His mother ran from the parlor, fear in her eyes. "Are you in pain?"

"No, Mother. I have a matter to settle with Nancy and Franklin."

"But, Sam, that's no way to call the servants. What's gotten into you, son?" She pressed her lips together in disapproval.

"I apologize, Mother." He kissed her on the forehead, and she reached up and patted his cheek.

"You called for me, sir?" Franklin stepped into the hall, and Nancy came scurrying in from the kitchen.

"I'd like to see you both in my bedroom as soon as possible. I have some questions." He turned to his mother, and when he spoke, his voice was gentle. "Mother, I'll be down for lunch. You don't need to send a tray."

He made his way slowly up the stairs, followed by Franklin and Nancy. When they reached the landing, Franklin stepped around him and went to open the door to Sam's bedroom.

When Sam was seated by the window, he looked up at Nancy first. "Please tell me again what you did with the letter you wrote for me last week. The one addressed to Miss O'Shannon at Ma Casey's Boardinghouse."

"Very well, sir. Like I told you, I sent for a messenger boy. But before he arrived, Cook needed me, so I gave the letter to Franklin and asked him to see that the boy got it." Fright filled her eyes. "Is anything wrong, sir? I wouldn't want to lose my position."

"If what you've told me is the truth, you have nothing to worry about, Nancy. You may go now. And thank you."

Sam watched her scurry from the room. Then he turned his gaze upon Franklin, who stood ramrod-straight, his eyes veiled.

"I'd like to know what's going on, Franklin. Why wasn't the letter delivered to Miss O'Shannon? If you misplaced it or forgot to give it to the messenger, that's quite understandable. You've been a loyal and trusted servant for many years. But I want to know the truth."

Sam watched as uncertainty followed by an expression almost like regret crossed the butler's face. When he spoke, it was respectful but firm. "I'm sorry, sir. I can't say."

Surprised, Sam looked at Franklin. "You can't or you won't?"

The elderly man hesitated then opened his mouth as if to speak but shut it again.

"Very well, Franklin. You may go."

Perplexed, Sam decided to send for a tray after all. He hadn't, however, counted on his mother bringing it up. "Mother, you didn't need to do that."

"And why not? I've brought you many a tray when you were a child. You're still my boy, you know." A twinkle in her eyes proved she wasn't upset with him anymore.

"How well I remember. Chicken soup was the meal of the day when I was sick. And also when I pretended to be sick to get out of the classroom."

She laughed. "And those times, it was followed by castor oil. A fitting punishment, I thought."

Sam grinned. "I don't think chicken soup or castor oil can fix what ails me now, Mother."

"I'm sure you're right. Affairs of the heart are not so easily cured."

He looked at her in surprise. "What do you mean?"

"You can't fool me, Sam. I know love when I see it. And perhaps unreturned love from the way you've been moping around."

Sam hesitated. Would she react the same way his father had? And suddenly, a chill went down his spine. His father had intercepted the letter. That's why Franklin was so secretive. Because his first loyalty was always to Sam's father.

"Sam, what's wrong?" His mother's startled voice brought him back from his thoughts.

He attempted a laugh. "I think I've just been overdoing it the last couple of days, Mother. I'm not really hungry. If you don't mind, I think I'll go to sleep."

"Of course."

After she left, Sam crawled between his sheets. Suddenly he really was tired. He leaned back on the soft pillows and closed his eyes.

The sound of footsteps woke him. He opened his eyes to see his father standing beside his bed.

"Are you awake?"

"Yes, what time is it?"

"Nearly six. Your mother said you've been sleeping for hours. Guess you needed it."

Carefully, aware of the ribs that were still not completely healed, Sam sat up, adjusting his pillows behind his back.

"I'm sorry, Sam."

Sam tensed. "Sorry about what?"

"I saw Nancy give the letter to Franklin and heard her tell him it was a letter for your 'young lady,' as she said." His father sighed, and Sam saw sorrow wash over his face. "What can I say except I'm sorry? I thought I was doing the right thing when I took it."

"You read it?"

"Of course not. I disposed of it." Shame filled his eyes. "I was wrong. I'm very sorry, Sam. I thought I was protecting you. Now that I've gotten to know so many of the Irish people, I've come to respect most of them. I asked around about Miss O'Shannon and heard about the good work she's been doing in the Patch."

Sam's chest tightened. He knew his father had thought he was doing the right thing, but could he forgive this outrage?

"Sam, all I can say is I'm so sorry and I'd love to meet the young lady. I just pray you can somehow forgive me."

With awe, Sam saw tears spring up in his father's eyes. Eugene Nelson, tough businessman, was crying.

He reached over and pressed his father's hand. "I do forgive you, Father. And I'm sure my Katie will be thrilled to meet you and Mother."

nineteen

Katie put on her best dress and then, peering into the mirror, arranged part of her hair on top of her head. She smoothed the ringlets hanging down on each side then picked up her hat and eyed it critically.

She'd purchased the plum-colored head covering from a catalog shortly before she came to the city. The lace and fake flowers were still as good as new. But the small black bird, which had so fascinated her at the time of purchase, now wanted to lean over onto the brim. She'd have to repair or remove it. But not today. After tugging the bird back into place, she arranged the hat on her head. It would simply have to do.

She'd been excited about church before, but this joy bubbling up inside her wasn't about sitting in the back pew, giggling with her girlfriends. She practically skipped downstairs and was surprised to see her pa, standing beside a smiling Rosie, wearing his best suit and smelling like pomade.

"It's about time you got down here, Katherine O'Shannon. And here we've been waiting for you fifteen minutes or more." He pulled out his pocket watch, gave it a quick glance, then replaced it in his vest pocket.

"Five is more like it, Michael. Don't pay him any mind, Katie. You're very pretty this morning. Isn't she?"

Katie grinned as her father took a closer look at her.

"Isn't that waist a little snug, daughter?" Creases appeared between his eyes.

"No, Pa, it's not snug in the least." She grabbed his arm. "Shall we go? I wouldn't want to be late."

They stepped out into the already scorching hot morning.

"My lands," Rosie said, holding a handkerchief to her face. "Were there more fires last night?"

"Hmm. It wouldn't surprise me any," Pa declared. "The count was at twenty for the week the last I heard."

Katie latched onto one of her father's arms while Rosie grabbed the other, and they headed down the street, turning when they reached the corner. By the time they reached the church, she noticed her father wheezed a little, and her own breathing was difficult as well.

A group of men stood on the steps outside the church, their conversation reaching to the sidewalk.

One man flung his arm upward. "That's right. The whole street's gone. Houses, stores, everything."

"What are they talking about, Father?" *Dear God, please don't let it be what it sounds like.*

Her father patted her hand. "Go inside, Katie. You, too, Rosie. I'll join you shortly."

She followed Rosie into the church, and they found seats in a pew about halfway up the aisle.

A smattering of women and children sat around the sanctuary, and an occasional whisper reached her ears.

Finally, the men drifted in.

Katie scooted over so her father could slide into the pew next to Rosie. "Father, what's going on?" She leaned over and peered around Rosie.

"Shhh." The sound came from the seat behind Katie.

A tall man had stepped onto the platform and made his way to the podium. He stood for a moment with his eyes closed. Was he praying?

"Brothers and sisters, neighbors," the deep voice sounded throughout the room, "some of you have heard about last night's fires. For those who haven't, I'm sorry to be the bearer of sad news."

A sob sounded from the other side of the room, and Katie heard a moan from farther back in the church.

"Four entire blocks were destroyed last night on the southwest side of town. I don't know the exact location, and I'm sorry I don't have more information. If you have family or friends in that area and would like to leave, we will be praying."

Katie averted her eyes as several people got up from their seats and hurried out. *Dear God. Help them. Let them find their loved ones safe.*

"If you'll bow your heads, I'll say a few words of prayer for those who may have lost homes or, worse still, family members." He paused a moment then sighed. "I'm afraid it's also time to pray for the safety of our entire city."

Katie closed her eyes and silently prayed, blinking back tears. Oh, why didn't it rain? *Lord, please send rain.*

"And now, if you'll open your hymnals, we'll continue our service with our brothers and sisters still in our hearts."

As Katie sang the familiar hymns, peace flowed into her spirit. She listened intently to the sermon that followed, almost awestruck. Grandma and Grandpa's church wasn't like this. Was it? If so, where was she at the time? In another world? Perhaps it was the tragedy and common-felt sorrow among the congregation that made it feel different. No, the feeling came from inside. Butterflies tickled her stomach. *God is really real.*

She had to cover her mouth and nose with her handkerchief during the walk home, as did her father and Rosie. She followed them into the house and went up to change into something fresh and lighter before dinner.

Why hadn't she invited Sam to dinner? Perhaps he'd drop by later. If not, the afternoon would drag. If only Bridget were here. But she wouldn't be home until sundown at least.

What could she do to make the time go faster? And get her mind off those poor people? As she walked into the hallway, the aroma of Ma's fried chicken wafted up the staircase. Her favorite meal. Her stomach churned. Who could eat?

Sam scanned the front page of the *Chicago Tribune*. His eyes rested on an article covering last night's fire. According to the reporter, the absence of rain had left everything so dry it would only take a spark to ignite the whole city. He shook his head. The southwest wind blowing off the prairie could make that prediction come true.

His mother came in from the kitchen and stopped in the middle of the room. "All anyone at church could talk about this morning was the fire and the possibility of more."

At the sight of her worried face, Sam got up and took her hands in his. "Now, Mother, don't be worrying yourself sick."

"I won't. I'm trying to lift it up to God." She offered a rueful smile. "Most of the time, I remember."

A twinge of guilt bit at Sam. How long had it been since he'd gone to church or even opened his Bible? He could remember a time when he was so close to God he could actually feel His presence. What had happened?

His mother placed her hand on his sleeve. "I'd like to talk to you before dinner."

She sat on the sofa, and Sam returned to his chair. "All right, Mother. What about?"

"Your father told me about Miss O'Shannon."

Sam's stomach tightened. "Yes? You know Father hasn't actually met her yet, and besides, he's given his permission for me to bring Katie to meet him."

"You don't need to sound so defensive, Sam. I'm not planning an attack." A dimple appeared and then hid again at her brief smile.

"You'll have to forgive me, Mother. I've been defending Katie to Father for some time."

"But I am not your father."

He darted a look at her. "Do you mean you approve? Even though she isn't one of your friends' daughters?"

"What do they have to do with anything? I want my son

happy, whomever he chooses to love. But as to whether I approve of your choice, I can't say. You haven't given me the opportunity to approve or disapprove."

Sam's jaw dropped open, and he burst out laughing. "You've a point there. I haven't, have I?"

She patted the seat next her. "So, come over here and tell me all about this girl who has managed to capture my son's elusive heart. Goodness knows I've thrown plenty of lovely young women your way with no success at all."

Sam sat where she directed and leaned back. How good it felt to relax when he spoke of Katie. "Mother, you will love her. I know you will. She's not only lovely to look at; she's sweet and kind."

Sam paused, wondering how to continue. How to show her the Katie he knew and loved. "Her parents were in vaudeville and lived in New York City. When she was fourteen, her mother died, and her maternal grandparents raised her after that. They have a little farm somewhere in southern Illinois. She turned eighteen a few months ago and came to live with her father."

"Tell me about him."

Sam smiled. "Michael O'Shannon is bigger than life with a stubborn streak and a heart of gold. He came here from Ireland when he was a small boy and is very much American. He's very protective of his Katie, and it took me quite awhile to win his trust so that I could call on her."

"What sort of acting does Katie do?"

"She won her first role after one of the other performers broke her foot. The actress is back now, so Katie only sings a solo before the show. Usually a ballad. She also helps out backstage."

"I always thought it would be exciting to be onstage." Her eyes sparkled.

Sam couldn't help the little choke of laughter at her words. "You, Mother?"

She flashed a smile at him. "I was a young girl myself once, you know. Of course, I'd have been locked up forever if I'd tried to follow that short-lived dream."

Franklin appeared in the doorway. "Dinner is served, Mrs. Nelson."

"Thank you, Franklin."

Sam fidgeted. Had he said enough? Too much?

Mother rose and waited for him then took his arm. "Ask Miss O'Shannon when it would be convenient for her to come to dinner."

A weight lifted off Sam, and he took a deep breath. "Thank you, Mother," he whispered.

"I've always wanted a daughter, you know."

Sam smiled at the dimple that appeared in her cheek.

&

Katie couldn't join in the festive mood with the rest of the troupe as Pat Devine entertained them with his fiddle. Why hadn't Sam come to see her? All right. So he didn't say he would be here today. But still. . .

She glanced at the mantel clock again. Seven. Bridget should have been here by now. Katie went to the window and peeked around the lace curtains and through the open window. With a huff, she sat on the wingbacked chair. Bridget wasn't coming either. She turned her attention to Pat, who had everyone in the room but her tapping their toes.

Rosie sat beside her. "Bridget's not here yet?"

"No. She must have decided to stay home tonight," Katie sighed.

"I know it's lonely for you with just us older folks for company." Rosie gave her an understanding smile.

"Oh no, Rosie. I love being with you." The older woman had been a wonderful friend to Katie. Almost like a mother.

"Mmm-hmm." Rosie gave her hand a squeeze. "We love you, too. But it's not the same as having someone your own age to talk to."

A shout of laughter drew their attention back to their boisterous friends.

Katie smiled at her father, who stood in the center of the room, surrounded by the others. "Rosie, they're insulting me."

"Now, you fellows, leave my man alone." Rosie gave a playful frown and went to stand by Michael, looping her arm through his.

Her man? Did Rosie call Pa "her man"? Katie put her hands to her cheeks. She'd known that Rosie had a crush on her pa, but when did he decide to return her affection?

Deciding she needed to collect her thoughts, she went outside and sat on one of the rocking chairs on the porch. The smoke from the night before seemed even stronger than it had earlier, probably carried by the wind blowing from the south. Like Pa said, the fire department was well equipped to take care of any more fires that broke out. Katie shivered. But then why did four city blocks burn to the ground?

Suddenly part of a verse from the minister's sermon came to her. *When thou walkest through the fire, thou shalt not be burned; neither shall the flame kindle upon thee.* What did that mean? People did get burned sometimes. Just last week, one of Harrigan's business associates had died in a fire.

Another shiver went through her body. She jumped up and hurried back to the parlor. Back to the noisy laughter. Back to where she was safe.

twenty

"Katie, wake up." Her father's voice broke through the sleep-filled fog. He shook her shoulder. "Katie."

"What's wrong?" She bolted upright, her eyes landing on her fully dressed father.

"More fires. Get dressed and come downstairs. We'll talk then." He rushed out. The door closed, and his running footsteps receded down the stairs.

Katie flung the covers aside, jumped out of bed, and grabbed the first dress her hands touched. She jerked it from the closet and threw it on over her shift and pantalettes. No time for a corset. Pa's voice sounded frightened.

Five minutes later, curls flying unconfined around her shoulders, she hurried downstairs. Voices sounded in the dining room. She hurried inside, finding the entire troupe there. "What's wrong?" She stopped and took a deep breath. "Is there fire heading this way?"

"Come sit down, daughter." Her father took her arm and led her to one of the straight-backed chairs by the table.

She looked at the small clock on the mantel. Ten thirty. No wonder she was so disoriented. She'd only slept a few minutes.

"Daughter, fire is out of control across the river. They're sayin' it started in someone's barn on DeKoven Street. The southern branch should stop it, but with all the oil floating on the surface, that's not certain."

She gasped. If the fire jumped that part of the river. . . "But the gasworks are near there. And, and. . ." *Conley's Patch and Bridget and. . .*

"I know, child." He patted her shoulder.

"What can we do?" Her knees weakened, and dizziness clouded her thoughts.

"A group is forming to help evacuate. Most of us men are going to join them. We'll be needin' your prayers."

"I'm going with you. I can't stay here when Bridget and her mother and Betty are in danger. And the children." She gasped. "They'll need all the help they can get over there, Father. Surely you can see that."

"She's right. I'm going, too."

Katie could have hugged Rosie. She sent her a grateful look.

"Now listen here, Katherine. I know you're worried about your friends, but you'll not be going, and that's that."

"Pa, please. Am I more important than those babies across the river?"

A look of anguish crossed his face. "No, but. . .you'll not be goin'."

"You have to let me go, Pa. God is able to protect me."

He stared at her as though memorizing every inch of her face. "All right, there's no time to be arguin'. But ya have to be careful. If ya see any sign of the fire getting close, get out of there."

Katie flinched at the panic in his voice. Was she doing the right thing? But she was supposed to go. She felt it deep inside.

"I'll take care of her, Michael." Rosie laid her hand on his arm. "I promise I won't leave her side."

Katie watched in awe as her pa stroked Rosie's cheek.

"And who will be takin' care of you, I'd like to know?" His voice broke.

"I will." Katie put her arm around Rosie's shoulder. "We'll watch out for each other."

"Here," Ma Casey's booming voice rang out as she walked into the room, her arms piled high with blankets. "Take these. If the fire gets bad, you can wet them down and wrap them around your heads and shoulders."

Dubious, Katie took one of the blankets.

She filed out of the door with Rosie and the rest of the troupe. They hurried to the theater and squeezed into Harrigan's three-seater carriage.

To Katie, the conveyance seemed to crawl down the board streets toward the river. Katie's stomach and chest were tight. The longer it took to get to the fire, the less time they had to help those in danger.

Rosie's hand moved under hers, and the older woman flinched.

Katie glanced down, realizing she was squeezing the life out of the poor woman's hand. "I'm sorry," she muttered, dropping the hand.

What if the fire had already jumped the river? They might run right into it. Could they outrun it?

Blocks away from the river, screams and the pounding of feet rose above the crunch and squeak of wagon wheels on the wooden street. Mr. Harrigan shook the reins. The horses sped up, the links on the harness and single trees jingling. They turned onto Clark Street. Terror filled the air. Mothers grabbed the arms of screaming children, pulling them onward. Men pushed carts filled with household goods. Barking dogs dashed among the human wave.

Katie peered forward to see if the fire was nearby. She could see flames in the distance, but they were still on the other side of the south branch.

"We'll never get the horse and carriage across the bridge," Pat yelled. "We'll have to go on foot."

Her heart pounding, Katie jumped from the carriage, still clutching the blanket Ma had pressed in her arms.

Harrigan unhitched the horse and slapped him on the rump. Startled, it whirled then took off.

"But. . .what about the carriage?" Katie whispered.

"Let's go." Rosie grabbed her arm and pushed her toward the bridge.

Katie forced her way through the crowd, her eyes glued to Rosie's back. Suddenly, a burly man pushed by and knocked her to the side. She stumbled, struggling not to fall. Disoriented, she looked around. A wall of bodies met her sight. Where was Rosie? And Father?

She shoved her way between elbowing, shouting people. *Oh God. Oh God.* Fear rose in her, and her heart raced. Finally, she found herself on the other side of the bridge.

"Miss O'Shannon!"

Even distorted with fear, the voice was familiar to Katie. Molly Sawyer. She looked around, but people blocked her view. Coughing and gasping, she pushed in the direction the voice came from. The crowd parted, and she saw Molly and her family. They stood by the dock, bundles tied to their backs about to step onto the bridge. "Molly, have you seen the Thorntons?" she yelled. She pushed her way through and grabbed Molly's shirt to stop her.

"They were still at home when I left. Out on their porch. Mrs. Thornton seemed in a daze. She wouldn't budge. Bridget was shakin' her and shakin her, but it didn't seem to do no good."

"Molly, what are you standin' there for? Come on!" Her husband grabbed her hand, and Molly turned and followed him onto the bridge. Instantly they were lost from sight in the crowd.

Frantic, Katie looked around. Flames roared just blocks away with only the south branch of the river containing it.

"Katie, over here!"

"Pa!" she cried out with relief as he grabbed her arm and pulled her to him. She held on as he led her to Rosie and the rest of the group who stood behind a small shed.

He turned and gazed at her. "We're crossing over the south branch to try to help those on the other side. You go with Rosie and look for your friends. Don't wait for us. God willing, the fire won't cross the main branch of the river, but

I don't want you waiting to find out. Do you hear me, Katie girl? Help those you can to get out of here and then head north."

She grabbed for her father. "No! Please! Don't go over there. It's not safe."

He gripped her hand. "Daughter! Pull yourself together. Trust God." Then he dropped her hands and was gone toward the flames.

She shuddered and took a deep breath. He was right. She swallowed to ease her smoke-sore throat. "God go with you," she whispered.

&

Sam stood by his father on the porch and watched the flames in the distance. "I can't tell exactly where it is, can you?"

"Not for sure, but it looks like it's near the river." He furrowed his brow and squinted.

Sam fidgeted. "Which side?"

"If you can't tell, how could I? Your eyesight's a lot better than mine." He continued to gaze eastward in the direction of the fire. "If it's on the east side of the south branch, the gasworks could go."

A knot formed in Sam's throat, and he swallowed. *If the gasworks blow, the Patch will be next.* "I think I'll ride down there. Check things out."

His father gave him a startled look. "Let me send Fred. You don't want to worry your mother."

Irritation shot through Sam. If he went himself, he could check on the Thorntons and the Flannigans. But his father was probably right.

A few minutes later, the coachman, lantern in hand, rode off on Fritzie, one of the bay mares that his father prized so.

Sam paced to the end of the porch. He stared eastward but could see no better than he had from his former position.

"Stop fidgeting. What are you so nervous about?"

"I have friends in Conley's Patch, remember?"

His father's face stiffened. "I'd forgotten. Well, chances are the fire won't reach them. I'd think the fire department should have it under control soon."

Sam gave a short laugh. "Like they did last night? The fire department has a scarcity of supplies, and such as they have are of inferior quality."

His father nodded. "I know, I know. I intend to address that at the next city council meeting."

Sam pulled out his watch and peered at the numbers. Ten minutes till twelve. Fred had been gone twenty minutes and should be back soon.

Katie. He dropped to the top step. Could she possibly be in any danger? The boardinghouse was north of the downtown district and should be fine as long as the fire didn't cross the main branch of the river. Still, a thread of concern planted itself firmly in Sam's mind.

The sound of hooves came from down the street. His head jerked in that direction.

Fritzie galloped up the street with Fred leaning forward, almost touching her flying mane. He yanked on the reins, bringing Fritzie to a stop in front of Sam, then swung from the saddle. "The fire's jumped the south fork! Oil on top of the water ignited. There was no stopping it."

Boom!

Sam grabbed his ears to protect them from the deafening explosion. The street and house lights flickered then died.

"What on earth?" his father bellowed from behind him.

Sam jumped to his feet. "That was the gasworks! I have to go." He ran down the steps and snatched the reins from Fred then swung painfully into the saddle. "Father, stay here, please. If the fire jumps the main branch, I'll check on the office. You stay with Mother."

Swinging Fritzie around, he headed east. Before he'd gone a quarter of a mile, he realized his mistake. Why had he thought he could get to the Patch this way with the fire converging on the area? He'd have to go around. He yanked on the reins, turned Fritzie, and then headed north.

Veering back east in the direction of the Patch, he galloped head-on into a mob. The panic shocked him. Shouts and screams rent the night. Men, women, and children, pushing carts and leading goats and cows, milled toward him. Time and again, he turned east, only to be turned back by a human mass that plunged forward into the night, with the fire a red backdrop in the distance.

"Ye half-wit! Why ye headed toward the fire?"

Two shadowy forms stood beside his horse. Sam peered at them in the darkness. The toothless old man gasped for breath and tightened his arm around his wife. The woman looked up, terror bright in her eyes.

"I have friends in the Patch. Has the fire reached there?"

"If it ain't yet, it soon will. The flames are a solid wall. It's gonta jump the main river soon. Bound to."

"God, help me. Show me what to do." Sam pressed his heels into Fritzie's side, and she quickened her step. What if the man was right and the main branch was breached? He had to get to Katie.

He steered Fritzie north again toward the business district. Smoke filled the air, biting his throat. He coughed. Fritzie tossed her head, snorting. Her ears turned back, and she reared up, her front feet pawing the air.

"Easy, girl." Sam patted her neck.

She relaxed a little, lowering her feet to the ground, but her ears remained back.

"It's okay." Sam patted her neck again. "We have to reach Katie." He swallowed and squeezed his legs tighter around Fritzie's sides to encourage her onward.

As he neared the business district, pandemonium filled the area. People stood in the streets in their nightclothes, hollering to each other. Demanding to know what happened to the lights. Had the fires reached them? Others ran from their homes clutching bundles.

Dear God, this whole city is a firetrap. There aren't more than two or three so-called fireproof buildings in all of Chicago. Tension tightened the muscles in his neck and stabbed at his chest.

Policemen strode up and down the street, shouting through cupped hands. "Everyone go back to your homes. There's no danger. The fire can't cross the main branch of the river."

A few people drifted back to their homes, but most ignored the police officers.

Sam urged Fritzie on, skirting the business district and finally arriving at Ma Casey's. He swung from the saddle, tore up the front steps, and banged on the door. Peering through the diamond-shaped window, he searched for Katie.

Ma Casey opened the door, holding a lamp high. Seeing Sam, she flung the door open.

He pushed past her. "Ma, where is everyone? Where's Katie?" He looked around. Surely they weren't sleeping through all the excitement.

"They've gone to help evacuate."

"What? Katie, too?" Fear surged through him. Surely Michael wouldn't have allowed her to go.

"There was no stopping her. Bridget didn't come home last night."

Dear God, please no. Katie at the Patch?

Leaping onto Fritzie's back, he whipped the reins and kneed her sides. She snorted but leaped forward. Through the business section. Onto Clark Street. The air heated as he went. Toward the bridge. He yanked the reins.

Horror hit him. A solid mass of screaming people flowed toward him. Behind them, a raging monster of flames, smoke, and debris licked at the banks of the river, swallowing up buildings, boats, everything flammable in its path.

"God, have mercy."

twenty-one

A red-hot ember flew over Katie's head and landed two feet in front of her. Sparks spewed up. Searing pain shot up her arm. She screamed and jumped to one side, tightening her hold on the tiny, squirming, crying child in her arms. The boards beneath the still-burning embers began to smolder.

"No!" The cry burst from her throat. Ashes rained down on them, coating the wet blanket she'd wrapped around the little girl.

"Katie, watch out!" Bridget's shout came from behind her.

She turned to see a bay horse, eyes rolling and hooves thrashing the air. She stumbled forward just as the horse's hooves crashed down on the spot where she'd stood.

"God, help us!" Mrs. Thornton's anguished cry was almost lost in the greater, almost solid sound of people, animals, and the roaring fire. Always the fire.

Katie clung tighter to her charge and ran with the fear-driven mob of people.

Betty, running hand-in-hand with Bridget, screamed a continuous scream.

Katie sobbed. *Sam.*

Lord, I trust You. Don't let me look back. The fire must be close behind.

Sam. Katie's neck and ears burned from the raging heat borne along with the wind. Her chest was so tight. She slowed her pace. If only she could stop but for a moment. *No. Don't think that.*

Sam.

God, help me. Help me run faster.

Glass shattered somewhere near, the sound assaulting her

ears. She turned to see a figure hurl itself from a third floor window. *Oh God.* She averted her eyes and ran on. The child was still, and no sound issued from the blanket. *Oh please, don't let her be dead. What if I've smothered her? Should I stop? No, I dare not.*

Sam.

Oh God, please don't let him search for me. Keep him safe.

No, I mustn't think of him. Concentrate on the child. Is she breathing? Don't think of anything but getting her to safety.

From somewhere came a burst of energy, and she quickened her pace.

Rosie. Where is Rosie? She was by my side when we crossed the bridge. I promised Father.

She took a deep breath and gasped. The air was getting hotter against her blistered skin and in her throat.

Shouts from behind. She threw a quick glance over her left shoulder. A building less than a block behind her was burning, its flames already licking hungrily toward the one next to it.

Oh God. Her legs and feet seemed to move of their own volition. Buildings at her side were aflame now.

The courthouse loomed before her. Then the lapping flames caught the dry, wood frame, and it began to burn. Men squirmed through windows on the lower floor and some jumped from the second floor. Suddenly a mass of humanity shoved through the doors, tripping over each other, trampling one another in their terror. They'd freed the prisoners. Thank God. They had a chance. Katie ran on.

More embers sailed through the air, falling all around. Screams of agony told Katie that some had landed on people.

Oh God, she prayed, unable to form any other words.

The crowd in front of her veered to the right. What were they doing?

"To the lakeshore," someone shouted. "It's our only chance."

Hope rose in Katie as she ran after the crowd. Of course.

They'd be safe on the shore of the lake. She ran faster.

Suddenly she couldn't feel her legs. A wave of dizziness hit her, and nausea rose in her throat. Her head began to bow. *God, I can't.* The blanket in her arms squirmed, and a hard kick landed on her side. She gasped and jerked upright. *Oh, thank You, God. She's not dead.*

Katie stared forward as she ran. Just a few feet more and she could rest. Her shoes hit sand, and she stumbled onto the edge of the water. Shouts and cries of relief pierced her ears, and she watched listlessly as people plunged into the lake, splashing water over blistered faces and necks. Katie's knees buckled, and she sank to the sand.

&

Fritzie screamed in terror and reared, her hooves lashing out.

Sam hung on, berating himself for bringing her into this. If he could get her to calm down enough, he could dismount. If he covered her head with something so she couldn't see the flying sparks or hear the roar of the fire that got closer every minute, he could lead her. Her hooves crashed down, and she sidestepped and reared again, her legs flying as she whirled in midair.

Sam hit the ground. Pain seared through his neck and shoulder. A braying, bucking donkey ran past him, followed by a large, barking dog. He stayed still until a wave of dizziness passed.

Bounding to his feet, he looked around for Fritzie.

"She took off." A young man with a cap perched sideways on his head yelled above the shouting people and mixed clamor of animal sounds. "I tried to grab her, but she was too wild. You shoulda seen the crowd make way for her. Scared 'em nigh to death."

"Thanks. Did you see which direction she went?"

"Nope. Crowd closed in behind her." The boy took off running.

Sam rubbed his shoulder and stood on tiptoe, hoping to

catch a glimpse of her. Nowhere in sight. Doubling his fist, he hit his other hand hard. What now? He had to find Katie. Had to keep her safe. According to a policeman, everyone had escaped the Patch before the fire got to it. Where would the troupe have gone?

A young woman stumbled and fell against him. A mewling sound came from the bundle she held in one arm. He caught her and steadied her, placing his hand against her back. She threw a look of hopeless fear his way and stumbled on, leaning heavily on a stick, her other arm holding tightly to the infant. Were they alone? A lame woman with an infant? She'd never outrun this fire.

He took one quick step and reached her. "Ma'am, would you allow me to help?"

She turned grateful eyes up to him. More than grateful. Maybe a little less than adoration. Now that he had a closer look, he realized she was younger than he'd thought. Probably not much older than Katie.

She stopped and the crowd rushed against them, almost knocking them apart. With a pleading look, she held the wrapped bundle toward him. Did she think he'd take the baby and leave her? His heart wrenched.

"No. You hold your baby." He reached down and picked her up in his arms, and the stick fell from her hands. He kicked it aside and took off running with the crowd. Embers flew over his head, and some landed near him.

Through the cacophony of sound, he heard a loud cry up ahead and looked that way. A body hurtled to the ground from a third floor window. His stomach churned, and he clamped his teeth together.

He was near the rear of the crowd. The flames roared like a train. Fiery heat burned his neck. The fire wasn't far behind. Screams sounded just behind him. He glanced back, and his heart lurched with fear. A building just a few yards behind him was engulfed in flames which reached out, threatening adjacent buildings.

He sped up with the crowd, and flames reached out to the buildings beside him, consuming them. The shrieking mob ahead turned toward the lake.

Shifting the woman in his arms, he ran after them. Pain stabbed his ribs. He gasped for breath as the smoky air filled his lungs.

The woman tugged on his shirt. "Please," she shouted. "I'm slowing you down. Take my babe and let me make my own way."

Ignoring her plea, he ran, stumbling as his weak ankle almost gave way. Gasping for air, he reached the edge of the lapping waves. The crowd pressed close around him.

"Make way," he yelled, wobbling where he stood. "I have a lame woman and her baby here."

People scattered to clear a small section of beach.

He set her gently on the sand and held on to her until she was seated with the baby in her arms. Then he fell to his knees, bending over, panting for air. He glanced over at his charges. The woman's head had fallen forward. Was she ill?

The mewling sound began again. Groaning, Sam pushed himself to his feet. He had to check on them. The mother's head jerked up, and she pulled the blanket from the baby's face. Sam inhaled sharply. A newborn. Very newborn.

He stooped down beside the woman and leaned close so she could hear his shouts above the crowd and the roar of the fire. "My name is Sam. Are you all right?"

She nodded and shouted, tears running down her ash-smeared cheeks. "Lucy Owens. God bless you, sir. You saved our lives."

"How old is your infant?"

Her face crumpled and tears filled her eyes. "He was born less than an hour before you found me."

"Do you have family?" He leaned closer to hear her better.

She shook her head. "My man died of the fever just three

months ago. There's no one but me. And him." She nodded at the baby.

"Are you lame or just weak?"

She blushed and ducked her head. "I'll be fit as a fiddle when I get my strength back."

Sam looked around, frustrated. He had to look for Katie. But he didn't feel right leaving Lucy alone. Heat and ash from the mile-wide fire fell on them as it raged past, less than a block away. *Dear Lord, please don't let it spread closer to the shore.*

"Sam Nelson, is that you?" The cry was followed by arms flung around his neck. She pulled away, and his eyes rested on the exhausted face of Rosie Riley.

૪ે

The child slept on the sand, one hand under her soot-coated cheek, oblivious to the terror and bedlam around her. Betty had fallen exhausted on the shore and lay motionless, covered by the damp blanket Bridget had thrown over her.

Katie leaned against a trunk and shut her burning eyes. The roar of the fire filled her ears. She forced them open. Why did it seem louder with them closed?

"Katie! Daughter!" She jumped up at the sound of her father's voice. His wonderful face was glowing, a smile stretching across his face as he ran toward her, followed by several members of the troupe, almost unrecognizable from the soot and ash. When he reached her, she fell into his arms, leaning against his strong, safe chest.

Now she could close her eyes. But immediately they flew open. "Pa, I'm so sorry. I got separated from Rosie. I don't know where she is." She hid her face in her hands.

She felt his hand gently remove hers from her face.

"Daughter, it's not your fault. The city is a madhouse. We'll trust God to keep Rosie safe."

"We'd just crossed the bridge when someone pushed this little girl into my arms. I looked around to see who it was, and when I looked back, Rosie was gone." She wiped at the tears that rolled down her cheeks. "Should I have searched for her, Pa? I had to get the child to safety, didn't I?"

He pulled her head back to his chest and patted her. "Of course, Katie girl. You did the right thing. Don't fret yourself now."

"Do you think Sam's all right? What if he's trying to find me? What if he got caught by the fire?" Panic clawed at her, like something wild attacking, draining her strength.

"Katie, stop it. You're imaginin' all sorts of things that aren't so. Sam can take care of himself. They're both in God's hands."

Katie swallowed and took a deep breath.

Of course, they were in God's hands. She had to stop falling apart like this. She stood straight. "I'm sorry. I'll be all right now."

Emma Gallagher knelt beside the sleeping child. "You don't know who she belongs to?"

Katie shook her head.

"Katie. Look."

At her father's excited voice, she glanced his way. Sam was running down the sandy beach, his face and clothing gray with ash, just as hers were.

Then she was in his arms, and he was holding her tightly.

"I couldn't find you. I searched everywhere and couldn't find you. I was so afraid." He held her at arm's length and stared into her eyes then pulled her to him again.

Her father cleared his throat, and Katie pulled away from Sam. She looked into his eyes and smiled.

Sam turned to her father. "Sir, Rosie Riley is down the beach. She's helping someone there. I told her if I found you, I'd let you know."

Katie watched joy brighten her father's face. He started off running down the beach, heedless of the wall of fire that had stretched closer to the shore, consuming building after building.

Tiny pieces of ash and debris floated on the wind. How close could the fire get to the lake? Would they be safe here?

Emma reached down and picked up the sleeping child. She trudged off across the sand.

Katie tugged at Bridget's arm. "Come. We have to go with Pa."

Bridget lifted Betty, and she and Mrs. Thornton dragged themselves after the others.

Sam took Katie's hand, and they tripped and stumbled across the sand through a red glow as Chicago burned.

twenty-two

Katie snuggled into the downy soft bed. She closed her eyes, and a satisfied sigh escaped from her throat. Wonderful.

The hot, sudsy bath had relaxed her tight muscles, and drowsiness washed over her. Could Bridget and Mrs. Thornton and that poor young mother be in as much heaven as she was? The kind housemaid who'd drawn her bath had laid a soft nightgown on the bed and told her she'd be back to help her out of the tub. Katie had almost laughed but didn't want to seem rude. She'd been taking her own baths since she was three and was quite capable of getting herself out of a bathtub.

Someone tapped on the door, but she was too tired to call out. She heard it open.

"Dear, do you mind if I come in?" The door closed.

Katie started and jerked from her reverie. Wide awake now, she glanced across at the white-haired woman standing by the door, her gentle smile resting on Katie's face. Katie drew in her breath sharply. She'd know those eyes anywhere. "Yes, of course." Her voice shook a little, and she cleared her throat.

Sam's mother stepped across the carpeted floor. "I hope you found your bath and bed to your liking." Her voice rippled like water over stones, gentle and singing.

"Oh yes, ma'am. Everything is wonderful. Thank you so much." She swallowed. "Please, would you like to sit down?"

The lady stepped to the wingbacked chair beside the bed and seated herself, smiling brightly at Katie. "I'm Mrs. Nelson. Sam's mother. And you are the lovely Miss O'Shannon."

Katie blushed. "Please call me Katie."

"Thank you. I believe I will." Wrinkles formed between her eyes. "I know you've been through a dreadful ordeal. Sam thought you might be concerned about your friends, so I came to tell you they are being cared for."

Relief washed over Katie. "Thank you. It's very kind of you to take strangers into your home."

"Nonsense. Any Christian soul would do the same." She gave a little nod. "The servants brought Sam's old cradle down from the attic, and our doctor has been here to care for the young mother. Lucy? I think that's her name. He says she needs bed rest but otherwise seems fine. Your friend Bridget and her little sister are sharing a room. Their mother is across the hall from them. They're all well but exhausted, with a few minor burns."

Katie felt the worry that had been nibbling at the back of her mind fade. "That's wonderful. I was a little worried. And the little girl I carried from the Patch?"

Mrs. Nelson lowered her eyes. "The doctor says she needs food and rest. She seems to have suffered neglect for quite some time." She sighed and looked into Katie's eyes again. "We've requested a nurse to care for her until she's well again. In the meantime, my husband and Sam will attempt to locate the parents. Then we shall see."

"The poor child. How old do you think she is?"

"The doctor says not more than two. Don't you worry. She'll be taken care of. And now you'd probably like to know your father has had his supper and is on the front porch with my husband, drinking lemonade. I think they might become fast friends."

"What about Rosie?" Katie had lost count of the times she'd thanked God for keeping her friend safe.

"Miss Riley has accepted the invitation of a member of the troupe whose home was out of the fire's path."

"Sam?"

A dimple appeared in Mrs. Nelson's cheek as she smiled. "My son has cleaned up and eaten an enormous dinner. He plans to join the men on the front porch after a while, as his father requested. But only after I assured him I would guard you with my life."

Katie gasped and blushed.

Laughing, Sam's mother stood. "My dear, you're just as precious as Sam told me you were. And now that I've made you blush, I'll get out of your way. Nancy will be here shortly with your tray. And you may sleep as long as you like." She stood and looked down at Katie, mist forming in her eyes. "It's quite easy to see why my son has fallen in love with you, my dear. And I must say I couldn't be more pleased."

"Thank you, Mrs. Nelson," Katie whispered, barely able to make any sound at all.

Mrs. Nelson gave her one last smile. "Good night, my dear. Tomorrow, we shall get to know each other." She walked softly to the door and left the room.

Sam had spoken of her to his mother. Not only that, Mrs. Nelson said he loved her. A thrill washed over her, and a spontaneous giggle sprang from her throat. Then another thought crossed her mind, and she sobered. What would his father think of her?

⠀⠀⠀⠀⠀⠀⠀⠀⠀⠀⠀⠀⠀⠀⠀⠀⠀⠀*

"Everything was black. The buildings. The ground. Ash falling all around." Sam's voice cracked. How could anyone convey the reality in words? He sat in a chair by his father on the front porch and watched the rain almost with disbelief. If it had only come earlier.

He gathered his thoughts and continued. "Father, you can't imagine what it was like. In moments, buildings, trees, everything incinerated."

He paused, reliving the horror. "We could feel the heat by the lake and had to dodge flaming debris as we watched Michigan Avenue demolished block by block."

He stopped and took a deep breath. Pain tore at his singed throat. "I'm sorry. Our building was reduced to rubble along with the others." Most of the factories along the river, including those belonging to Jeremiah Howard, had burned to the ground. No one had heard from him since the fire, not even his wife, so he was assumed dead.

"A lifetime of work for us and so many of our friends—gone in an instant." His father sighed loudly. "However, we have other things to attend to for now. We'll talk about rebuilding in the days ahead."

"I wasn't sure how you'd feel about my bringing my friends home with me."

"I'm not totally heartless, Sam." He frowned. "Did you see any sign of the Flannigans?"

"None. Katie said they left their home at the same time as she and the Thorntons. They got separated somewhere along the way. I can only hope they made it to safety."

"We'll find them."

Sam relaxed. They'd find them.

"I'm pleased that Miss O'Shannon is safe."

Sam darted a look at his father.

"Harrumph." His father cleared his throat loudly. "She's welcome here. As your friend. As your bride."

A heavy weight lifted off Sam. *Thank You, Lord.*

"I can't tell you how happy you've made me, Father. I plan to speak with her father. With his blessing, I'll ask her to marry me at the earliest opportunity."

"I suspected as much. Let me be the first to congratulate you."

Sam laughed. "She hasn't accepted me yet."

Hooves pounded up Prairie Avenue. A horse and rider galloped up the driveway and stopped in front of Sam and his father. The horse's wet sides heaved.

"Mr. Nelson, I've a letter for you, sir." He reached into a saddlebag and produced a long, thin envelope.

"Thank you." Sam took the letter and handed it to his father. "Can you give us any information about the damage?"

"Reports are starting to come in. Just about everything on the southeast side of town is gone. Then a mile-wide path from the river all the way to the far north. Seventy-three streets, that's what I'm hearing. Many of the bridges are gone. The business district is all but gone. Post office, Palmer House Hotel, just about everything." He shook his head, and his eyes looked dazed. "Don't know what's gonna happen."

"We'll rebuild, of course."

Admiration for his father rose up in Sam. He just hoped when he saw the devastation with his own eyes he'd remain optimistic. "Do you know how they finally stopped the fire?"

"Some buildings had to be blown up. After that, there wasn't anything left but a little prairie grass. The fire still tried to keep going. But when the rain started, it kind of burned itself out in the old graveyard." He sat up straight in the saddle and stretched. "I have to go. More of these to deliver."

Sam watched his father rip open the envelope and scan the letter. "They've already started making plans to help the homeless. The mayor has called a meeting for in the morning to discuss the situation. Homeless are our priority. Of course, the city waterworks is gone. It'll take awhile to get it operating again. Those of us with wells should consider ourselves very fortunate."

❧

Katie looked over her shoulder at Bridget as she pinned a sheet to the clothesline. "Would you bring me that basket? This one's empty."

Three weeks after the fire, the Nelsons were now hosting over a dozen people, including the babies. Which made for a lot of meals, dirty dishes, and of course, dirty laundry. The servants couldn't keep up with it all, so all the women except for Lucy, who was still weak after months of nearly starving while trying to keep her unborn child alive, insisted on helping.

Sam had initially protested when he saw Katie bending over a washtub, but when his mother walked up and plunged her manicured hands into the rinse water, cheerfully singing at the top of her lungs, he threw his hands in the air and walked away.

Katie finished hanging the sheets and went inside. Sarah Flannigan was coming out of the door with rugs slung over her arm. She smiled and ducked her head as she passed Katie.

Fred, the coachman, had found the Flannigans three days after the fire, living in a tent among rows of others. Mr. Nelson insisted the man who'd cared for Sam the night of the attack wasn't living in a tent and they must accept his hospitality until a proper house could be constructed for them.

The gesture solidified Katie's love for the man who raised Sam. It was easy to see the man she loved came by his kindness naturally.

That evening, she headed for the kitchen to help with dinner when Sam walked in the front door. A lock of hair had fallen onto his forehead. His eyes lit up as they met hers. He smiled that smile that made her knees go weak. Her heart pounded. Why did it have to do that every time he was near? Hastily she reached up to rescue the curls that had slipped from the long braid that hung down her back.

"How's the building coming along?" A nice safe subject. She hoped her father wasn't working too hard on the construction that had provided jobs for all who wanted to work. He wasn't getting any younger and wasn't used to that kind of work. But what was he to do? The troupe had disbanded until the theater could be rebuilt, and as he'd told her sternly, he wasn't about to be anyone's charity case.

"I can't believe how much has been accomplished in less

than a month." He smiled. "Maybe Chicago will thrive again."

Mrs. Nelson came into the hall. Her eyes sparkled as she glanced from Sam to Katie. "How would you two like to share a pot of tea with me on the porch?"

Katie nodded as Sam threw a questioning glance her way. She went to get the tea then joined Sam and his mother on the porch. She set the tray on a small wrought iron table. Sam motioned her over to the swing where he sat. His mother rested on a wicker chair across from them.

"Doesn't the air feel lovely?" Excitement trilled in Mrs. Nelson's voice.

"Yes, ma'am." In spite of everything, the autumn air was now crisp and fresh. Katie smiled. "Sam told me how much you love autumn."

Mrs. Nelson nodded and smiled. "It's my favorite time of the year. You know, I've been thinking we should have a party."

"A party? With the city in shambles?" Sam lifted an eyebrow. "Who would come?"

"Don't be foolish. Everyone will come. We'll do a benefit auction with a ball to follow. It will do wonders for the citizens of this city." Mrs. Nelson picked up her cup and stood. "Well, I think I'll have my tea inside after all. It's getting a little cold for me. You two stay."

Katie stared in astonishment as Sam's mother went inside and closed the door, leaving them in the dark. Katie glanced at Sam.

He gave her a tender smile and took her hand, rubbing his thumb across it.

She shivered.

"Sweetheart, don't mind her. She's always wanted a daughter."

Warmth washed over her. He'd called her "sweetheart." And "daughter"? What was he saying? Did he mean. . .

"Katie, I'd planned to do this differently, in a more romantic setting, but. . ."

Her heart raced, and she looked into his warm brown eyes. Eyes filled with love for her.

"I spoke to your father last night and received his blessing." He swallowed, slid off the swing, and knelt down on one knee in front of her.

"You must know how I feel about you. From the first moment you lifted those big blue eyes in the train station, I've been unable to think of anything but you. I love you, sweetheart. And it would give me the greatest joy if you'll agree to be my wife." He reached into his pocket and removed a small velvet box. The lid sprang open, and she gasped.

"Katie, this ring belonged to my maternal grandmother. I hope with all my heart you'll wear it. Will you marry me?"

"Oh, Sam," she whispered, "I love you, too. And to be your wife would be the most wonderful thing I can imagine. It will be an honor to wear your grandmother's ring."

Her hand tingled as he slid the ring on her finger. She held up her hand and looked at the sparkling gems as he sat beside her. "It's the most beautiful ring in the world."

"When I told Mother of my intentions, she insisted that you must have it."

"Oh, I must go and thank her!" Katie shifted but found herself locked in a warm embrace as Sam's arms encircled her, pulling her close.

"There'll be plenty of time for that," he whispered, lowering his head.

Katie's stomach dipped, and she raised her head willingly for his kiss.

A Letter To Our Readers

Dear Reader:
In order that we might better contribute to your reading enjoyment, we would appreciate your taking a few minutes to respond to the following questions. We welcome your comments and read each form and letter we receive. When completed, please return to the following:

Fiction Editor
Heartsong Presents
PO Box 719
Uhrichsville, Ohio 44683

1. Did you enjoy reading *A Girl Like That* by Frances Devine?
   ❑ Very much! I would like to see more books by this author!
   ❑ Moderately. I would have enjoyed it more if

   _____

   _____

   _____

2. Are you a member of **Heartsong Presents**? ❑ Yes ❑ No
   If no, where did you purchase this book? _____

   _____

3. How would you rate, on a scale from 1 (poor) to 5 (superior), the cover design? _____

4. On a scale from 1 (poor) to 10 (superior), please rate the following elements.

   ____ Heroine   ____ Plot
   ____ Hero   ____ Inspirational theme
   ____ Setting   ____ Secondary characters

5. These characters were special because? _____

_____

_____

6. How has this book inspired your life? _____

_____

_____

7. What settings would you like to see covered in future
   Heartsong Presents books? _____

_____

_____

8. What are some inspirational themes you would like to see
   treated in future books? _____

_____

_____

9. Would you be interested in reading other **Heartsong
   Presents** titles? ☐ Yes ☐ No

10. Please check your age range:
    ☐ Under 18   ☐ 18-24
    ☐ 25-34   ☐ 35-45
    ☐ 46-55   ☐ Over 55

Name _____

Occupation _____

Address _____

City, State, Zip_____

CHASING CHARITY

Charity Bloom's heart is torn between two men—a handsome roughneck and a deceitful rogue. Who will win her treasured heart?

Historical, paperback, 304 pages, 5³⁄₁₆" x 8"